# Some Like It Cold

It was a procurer's dream. Freeze the girls now, thaw them later to fill an order. . . .

"On the table they've got this beautiful young girl. She's tied down and just as naked as the day she was whelped. A real knockout. They actually killed her, right there while everyone watched. They shut off her oxygen and then, when she was dead, they hooked her up to a heart and lung machine and all sorts of gadgets and needles and jazz, and then had me start to bring down the temperature in the room. Gradual, they said, and before they were done, that knockout of a girl was frozen stiff as an icicle on a barn roof in the middle of winter."

## THE PENETRATOR SERIES:

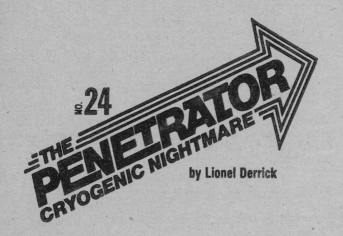

# THE PENETRATOR

## No. 24

## CRYOGENIC NIGHTMARE

by Lionel Derrick

PINNACLE BOOKS                    LOS ANGELES

This is a work of fiction. All the characters and events portrayed in this book are fictional, and any resemblance to real people or incidents is purely coincidental.

PENETRATOR #24: CRYOGENIC NIGHTMARE

*Copyright © 1978 by Pinnacle Books, Inc.*

An original Pinnacle Books edition, published for the first time anywhere.

Special acknowledgment to Chet Cunningham

ISBN: 0-523-40177-9

First printing, February 1978

Cover illustration by George Wilson

*Printed in the United States of America*

PINNACLE BOOKS, INC.
One Century Plaza
2029 Century Park East
Los Angeles, California 90067

# Contents

# CRYOGENIC NIGHTMARE

# PROLOGUE

FBIWASHDC SENDING
ALL POINTS RESTRICTED MATTER **\*\***
NEED TO KNOW DISTRIBUTION ONLY. CLEAR
CIRCUIT.
FROM: H. GOODMAN #104–33USFBI
TO: UNIFORM CRIME NETWORK, USDOJ, ALL LEA,
INTERPOL.
SUBJECT: THE PENETRATOR, ALIAS JOHN SAVAGE,
PHIL BURRITT, JUDSON DEER, ETC. FEDERAL WARRANTS
OUTSTANDING FOR: INTERSTATE FLIGHT, MURDER,
DESTRUCTION FEDERAL PROPERTY, KIDNAPPING,
ARMED ROBBERY, MANY OTHER FEDERAL, LOCAL
CRIMES.
PARTIAL DESCRIPTION: HAIR, BLACK. EYES, BROWN OR
BLACK. COMPLEXION, DARK. RACE, CAUCASIAN,
MIXED.
SUMMARY WITNESS REPORTS: HEIGHT: 6-2 TO 6-4,
ABOUT 220 POUNDS, BODY SHOWS 12 TO 15 WOUNDS
FROM KNIFE, BULLET. AGE 26 TO 30.
OPERATES ALONE. NO KNOWN FINGERPRINTS OR PHOTO.
ARMED AND EXTREMELY DANGEROUS.

1

USUALLY GOES TO CRIME HOT SPOTS AROUND NATION, WORLD. SOMETIMES DESCRIBED AS MODERN ROBIN HOOD FIGHTING MOBSTERS, TERRORISTS, THOSE TAKING ADVANTAGE OF WEAK AND OPPRESSED. DOES NOT FIRE ON LEGITIMATE POLICE, LAW OFFICERS. TRADEMARK, 2-½ INCH-LONG CHIPPED, BLUE FLINT ARROWHEAD LEFT ON VICTIMS TO STIR TERROR IN ENEMIES. M.O. INDICATES VIETNAM SERVICE EXPERIENCE. MASTER OF ALL MILITARY HAND WEAPONS, GRENADES, EXPLOSIVES. IF YOU HAVE INFORMATION ABOUT SUBJECT NOTIFY THIS OFFICE AT ONCE FOR ASSISTANCE. DO NOT MAKE CONTACT WITH SUBJECT! TWENTY-MINUTE RESPONSE BY THIS OFFICE TO TELEX INQUIRY ABOUT SIGHTING OR INFORMATION ABOUT PENETRATOR, HIGHEST PRIORITY THIS DEPARTMENT. ATTENTION: HOWARD GOODMAN. GOODMAN #104–33USFBI SENDS.
EOM


POLICE BUSINESS****
OPEN MESSAGE.
FROM: DENVER PD #138–413J PARNELLI.
TO: GOODMAN #104–33USFBI WASHDC
***IMMEDIATE ATTENTION, GOODMAN***
RE: THE PENETRATOR—LOCATION.
SUBJECT INVOLVED THIS AGENCY THURSDAY LAST. PARTICIPATED IN BREAKUP OF "CHURCH OF FINAL COMING," AND PROPHET VANUA LEVU. CHURCH UNDER

SUSPICION LONG TERM AS RUNAWAY HAVEN,
PROSTITUTION, DRUG OUTLET. DPD AGENTS VANISHED
THERE. EXTENT OF PENETRATOR INVOLVEMENT IN
DESTROYING CHURCH NOT KNOWN. RESCUED TWO
TEEN-AGE GIRLS, RELEASED MANY OTHERS. SEVERAL
KNOWN WANTED MEN DEAD IN ACTION. NO WARRANTS
HERE FOR PENETRATOR. NO TRACE OF HIM. NO
PRINTS, NO SOLID DESCRIPTION. BELIEVE HE LEFT
AREA SHORTLY AFTER DESTRUCTION OF TEMPLE.
COMPLETE DETAILS INVOLVING SUBJECT AND ALL DPD
REPORTS OF ACTION IN MAIL YOUR ATTENTION
THIS DATE.
PARNELLI #138–413J SENDS.
EOM

Willard Haskins ex-geology professor at USC, laid
down the telex paper and sighed. Another hunter was
on the trail. This one seemed to have little more information or hard evidence about Mark than the others; still it was a worry. It would be a tragedy if some
federal lawmen trapped Mark and he had to stand
trial for the good work he was doing. No! The Penetrator must be protected at all costs. He had gone into
battle almost two dozen times now, fighting for the
little guy, for the down-and-outer, for the honest cop
and politician. These missions had been against terri-
ble odds, with the hoodlums and police both often
trying to eliminate the Penetrator.

And so far, Mark Hardin, known now in many
parts of the world as The Penetrator, had charged
through and won each time, despite the odds, but often he paid a tremendous physical and mental price.

3

It had been several years now since the professor met Mark as a just-discharged veteran who had been broken up in Vietnam, not by the enemy, but by a small self-serving clique of army extremists who hated him for exposing a giant military goods black market in Saigon. He had come to the desert on the advice of his old UCLA football coach and a good friend of Professor Haskins. Once there he mended in the southern California sun in the Calico mountains near Barstow. The professor had built an ecologically perfect hideaway in the vaulted rooms of an old borax mine and, what little work that was done on the surface was built in, blended and camouflaged with the surrounding desert and bluffs so the Stronghold was almost impossible to find. That was the idea.

At the Stronghold, Mark met the ancient Cheyenne, David Red Eagle. He told Mark he was half Cheyenne and took Mark under his tutorship, teaching him all of the old-time Indian ways of survival, of desert fighting, religion, medicine and body conditioning. Each time Mark returned from a battle, the old Indian put Mark on a regimen to get him healthy again and to build up his strength to a fighting pitch.

Professor Haskins served as research and outside contact man, utilizing his hundreds of loyal students and colleagues around the nation to gain special information on almost any subject, including data on criminal problem areas. The professor had a dozen such situations on the planning board in his study. Some were worsening to the point they would need attention soon. The professor hoped that this latest FBI bulletin to all law enforcement agencies in the

4

nation did not trigger any police or FBI trouble for Mark.

The cover name of John Savage was useless now. Usually such a cover was good for one operation only, since the local police and FBI men debriefed everyone after any contact with a man who even *might* be the Penetrator, and names were hard to protect. The professor was pleased, however, with the way most of these strangers had helped shield the vital description of the Penetrator. Most who were in close contact with Mark realized his essential purpose and knew he was a protector. They would not violate that trust and his help to them by giving out a clear and solid description of him.

This whole crime fighting work had begun several years ago. Mark had just come to the Stronghold, and the professor's niece had been there for a vacation. She and Mark had fallen desperately in love and together they probed Mark's background in some Los Angeles county records. Without knowing it, they stumbled into some secret organized crime activity, and the hit men moved in and forced Donna's car off the road and down a steep cliff. Mark was thrown out of the car, but Donna died in the flaming wreck.

That same week, Mark, the professor and David Red Eagle made a pact to strike back at the crime leaders who had killed Donna. Mark hit them hard and fast, almost obliterating the Mafia Family in Los Angeles, and scooping up the $450,000 in hoodlum money. With the money they decided to launch a nation-wide crime-fighting operation, striking at criminals anywhere who took advantage of the people. They had been fighting ever since.

The professor went to his activity board and

checked it. The three-foot high by four-foot wide wall map of the United States with Hawaii and Alaska inserts held nearly a dozen small red flags. Twenty green squares showed where the Penetrator had already swung into action. Two areas had large red explosion stickers: these were the current and most volatile problems. The hottest centered in a small Florida town where a man lived who had been on the professor's list of "interested citizens" for over three years. For all that time the professor had gathered information, collected data, and gathered police and FBI reports on one of the biggest and toughest of the independent organized crime figures in America— Preacher Mann. He was not tied in with any Mafia operation; instead he had singlehandedly built his own organization that extended into a dozen states.

Joanna Tabler and Mark were at the Islandia Hotel in San Diego getting caught up on their fishing out of Mission Bay's Islandia Marina on their chartered cruiser. The professor hated to break up their vacation, but Joanna's boss in the Justice Department had telephoned three times in the past two days demanding to know where Joanna was. And the professor knew it was past time to show Mark the two latest trouble spots and see if he thought it was time to pick out his next target.

Professor Haskins settled down in his big leather chair behind his mahogany desk and phoned a message to Mark, at the Islandia hotel in San Diego. It said: "Lots of live squid bait and yellowtails are biting. Ready to go fishing?" He signed it, simply, Willard. That should provoke some action, and very soon the Penetrator would be on the prowl again.

## Chapter 1

## NOT REALLY DEAD

Mark Hardin stood beside his Beechcraft Duke in the edge of the hangar at the West Palm Beach airport, his senses alert, every nerve ending straining to pick up exactly what was bothering him. But he couldn't. He watched the completion of the turnaround servicing on his plane, making sure it was all done exactly right. Still it was there, a vague uneasiness, a dryness in his nostrils, that certain indefinitive, gut feeling that something was wrong.

But Mark's grin was as wide as always. He had landed about an hour before and transferred his two identical suitcases from the Duke into a rented Granada. One of the cases held his clothes and traveling equipment. The other aluminum bag carried his armament, enough to launch a small war and plenty to get him arrested on the spot for weapons violations.

The Penetrator watched the service man, who had taken his time. He was a tall, thin youth with sandy hair and lots of freckles who couldn't be over nineteen or twenty, but knew his work. His grin was as wide as Mark's and maybe that was one of the problems that alerted Mark. The kid tossed the keys to Mark and cleaned his hands on a blue wipe rag.

"Guess you'll want to take one final check before you lock her up," the kid said. "Don't blame you, she's a real sweetheart of a ship."

The alarm bells were going off again. Had Mark ever seen this person before? Why did the slender youth seem familiar yet there was nothing in Marks mental file? Or was this a type, the kind of a flip, wise, loud mouth he ran into all the time, and didn't especially like? Only this time there seemed to be something else, something cloaked, hidden, just under the surface, and Mark couldn't unmask it.

"Yeah, thanks for a good job," Mark said, handing the sandy-haired youth a five-dollar bill. The boy took the bill without checking the denomination and shoved it in his pocket.

"Thanks, man. Have a good vacation," he said, took one more look at Mark and walked back to the hangar office at the far end of the big structure.

Mark spent half an hour more checking over his plane, then looked at the small envelope of vital information he had on his subject before he folded it and pushed it into his shirt pocket. In honor of the warm weather, Mark wore light-weight blue slacks and a matching shirt with wild birds printed on it. He almost *looked* Florida. The sandy-haired kid was gone. Mark doublechecked the ship again, still uneasy, but got into his Granada and drove out of the hangar.

He paused outside again, trying to remember if he had ever seen the youth before. Early, it seemed way back, Los Angeles? Mark pushed it aside, and drove toward the airport entrance. He thought of going into the terminal to the dining room, but decided instead that he would get his motel room, take a long, hot shower and then a leisurely dinner before he got to work. It was a little after three P.M.

Mark pulled to a stop at the airport entrance light and turned onto the main roadway angling for West Palm Beach. It had been good to get a chance to stretch after the long hours of flying. He caught a flash in his rear-view mirror and saw a light blue Caddy rip through the red light, slam fast across traffic and settle into the lane behind Mark. The Penetrator turned slowly into the outside lane, leaving the fast strip open for the Caddy in a rush.

A moment later the big blue car had not passed him, and Mark checked his rear-view mirror and saw the Cadillac cruising along three car lengths behind him. Why had it been in such a rush, but now was content to hang back?

The itching at the back of his neck increased and Mark knew it was trouble. The sandy-haired kid had been a ringer, and the car behind was not out for a pleasure drive. The tail was poorly done, so obvious and amateurish that they must want him to run, chase him into the outback swamps somewhere. No way he could outrun that Cadillac. Mark speeded up suddenly to fifty-five miles per hour and the tail stayed. He slowed to twenty-five and the blue car was still there. Ahead Mark saw a pull-out space along the road beside a shallow ditch filled with water.

This was as good a place as any. He loosened the .45 caliber Star automatic in the clip-on holster hidden under his sport shirt and turned the Granada

9

onto the pull-out gravel. Suddenly the Caddy behind him spurted ahead, and Mark saw glints of three gun muzzles pointing out the passenger side windows. Mark hit the brakes, skidding and turned the wheel so the car's rear end would swing toward the ditch, then he dove for the floorboards. The Granada kept sliding until the nose of his car was aimed at the highway, putting the engine between Mark and the two .44 magnums and the shotgun loaded #00 buck. The guns all went off repeatedly, and Mark heard the rain of lead slamming into the Granada and through it. The bullets punched a dozen holes in the car, shattering the windshield, and Mark realized that the only thing that saved his skin was the Granada's engine block and firewall in front of him. The car kept skidding, hit the edge of the ditch, pitched over and rolled onto its roof where it stopped. It was a gradual roll and Mark found himself on the inside of the car's roof looking out the windows, both of which had been opened and now were half covered with the ditch water. Mark heard the Caddy skid to a stop on the road and begin to back up. He moved to the side of the car away from the roadway and pushed out through the window half filled with water. Outside of the car he lay in the ditch in which grew hundreds of shoots of heavy grass and water reeds of some kind. They half concealed the car. He heard the Caddy stop and knew he had to get away.

Quickly, but with no noise, Mark began pulling himself through the water deeper into the thick cover of the reeds. He made it a dozen feet from the car, staying on the far side of the ditch where the reeds were heaviest, and the wind blowing the reeds covered his movement.

Men talked, argued. "For Christ's sake, do it, somebody's coming!" one man shouted.

Mark kept working silently through the foot-deep water, half floating, half dragging his prone body through the concealing reeds until he couldn't hear the voices anymore. Then the ditch convulsed, as what sounded like an old Korean war fragmentation grenade exploded inside the Granada. Then another similar small bomb went off and Mark heard a piece of shrapnel whine past him through the reeds. A moment later he smelled smoke and saw the flames. He moved quickly now along the ditch.

He had no idea who the men were in the Caddy, but it had to be tied in with the sandy-haired youth at the hangar. What the hell was going on, anyway? Who was trying to burn him down an hour after he got into the state? Nobody even knew he was coming here but the two men at the Stronghold. He sat down in the water and listened as the Caddy engine purred and doors slammed. Then gravel spurted from tires and Mark lunged through the reeds toward the roadway. He drove his head through the last bit of screening and caught the license plate as the Caddy flashed past, laying rubber on the blacktop as it shot down the highway. It was a Florida number—FA-0951. Mark slotted it into his memory bank for future reference. Then he moved back to the far side of the ditch and found that the reeds were tall enough here that he could walk and not be seen. He moved through the wet for what he guessed was a half mile, then came out on the field side of the ditch and tried to get clean. Somewhere in the melee he had lost his .45. He took the clip-on holster off his belt and pushed it into his rear pocket, then he combed his dark hair

11

and took off the light-weight shirt and wrung it out, letting it hang over some weeds in the sun fifteen minutes until it was dry.

When he walked into the filling station a half mile further up the road he used the telephone and ordered another rental car, this one from Avis, using his second set of identification. He said he'd pick up the car at the airport in a half hour.

Mark used the filling station's restroom to clean himself up a little more, but knew there was nothing he could do about the pants.

He didn't have any trouble at the Avis counter but, when he walked away, the counter girl lifted her brows in surprise. He picked up the car and drove slowly back to the hangar where his plane was. Mark checked at the little office but no one was there. He slid in and took out his identical back-up aluminum bags from the Duke and locked it again and drove away, he hoped before anyone noticed. In the airport men's room he changed clothes and washed up again. He looked halfway presentable. Now he wore all white—shoes, pants and a white sport shirt that covered his clip-on holster and spare small-sized Star .45 on his belt.

Outside, Mark checked his car, then drove the Dodge Monaco out of the airport and toward a cluster of people and cars around his wrecked Granada. He stopped behind a dozen other cars and walked up to the site. Four policemen stood there warning people away from the wreck.

"Folks, this car evidently had some live ammunition in it, and the fire isn't out. A shell explodes now and then, so please stay back."

People moved back, then edged forward. The

Granada had been burned out. It still rested on the roof; no attempts had been made to put out the fire. One of the tires still burned, sending up a trail of black smoke into the cloudless sky.

As he watched the Granada, Mark tried to figure out how it could have happened. He pulled his big sunglasses on, the ones with lenses that hid half his face, which worked as a fine disguise, and walked back toward his Monaco. No one knew he was coming here, so that meant somebody made a positive I.D. on him the first hour he was in town. Who? The rental girl? Hardly. The airport tower? No way. It had to be the sandy-haired kid at the hangar. Was he a plant? He was at the transient hangar, and would see most of the private planes coming through there for fuel, servicing or layover. So somebody was watching for a Duke and a big guy, dark like him. He'd shaved off the moustache months ago, and wore his hair differently now. Maybe he'd have to go to a blond wig and a full beard.

Before Mark left the wreck site one cop had been asking another one if the driver had been taken out. The other officer had shaken his head. "You want to go in there and get his fried guts with them rifle rounds going off all the time? We'll get his burned pelt out of there after it cools itself down."

Mark got in the Monaco and drove to a fine motel he remembered from a trip through here before, the Sea Breeze. It fronted the water and had a good restaurant. He checked in under his Johnnie Denver I.D., which he had used to rent the second car, and once in the room, dropped on the bed.

Something kept probing at his memory, stirring up the circuits, activating old input data, mixing it and

13

sorting. Los Angeles; no, Las Vegas. Yes, Las Vegas and the Fraulein and that sin trap, the Pink Pussy Casino. Hadn't there been a bunch of young kids working the sidewalk outside—"pullers," they were called—talking people into coming into the clubs? They were too young to work inside but on the sidewalk it was legal enough, fifteen, sixteen.

Then Mark remembered, he had come face to face with the kid, not once, but two or three times in his action around the Pink Pussy Casino. Once he had to push him out of the way and the kid had snarled at him and tried to pull a knife but Mark had slapped it away and put him on the sidewalk with two quick, half-pulled karate blows. The boy had cried and swore he'd get even.

Mark remembered him well now, and superimposed that face on the grin of the sandy-haired youth at the hangar. They matched! Somehow that snot-nosed kid from Las Vegas had tied up with a hardcase, one who wanted eye-ball protection from the Penetrator, and he certainly had made a good investment. This "Sandy" could be dangerous and whoever he worked for was more dangerous.

Now he had a double task. Find out who Sandy worked for, and then move in on the Preacher Mann.

## Chapter 2

## BADMAN, PREACHER MANN

On the tenth floor of a big downtown West Palm Beach office building, Preacher Mann welcomed his evening meal, a high protein, vegetarian plate specially prepared in his own kitchen by a vegetarian chef. Preacher's real name was Peter Doxford Mann, he was thirty-six years old, negroid, six-feet four inches tall and weighed two hundred and forty pounds. He ate six meals a day and was superbly conditioned, swam a mile a day, and worked out another hour on a punching bag and in his weight room.

The Preacher was totally bald, had his head and face shaved each morning. His skinhead emphasized huge jug-handle ears and large brown eyes. His nose had flaring nostrils over thick lips.

When he finished eating, he pushed the tray away, drank the rest of the quart of orange juice, and put the thirty-two-ounce glass on the tray, then waved it all away.

"Now, bring in this Las Vegas eyeball I've been

paying so much all these months, and let's see if he's worth it." A black man nodded, took the tray, and hurried out.

Preacher Mann sprawled on a low couch made of eight separate pieces of upholstered furniture that fitted together into a huge square. Over it was a satin spread of deep purple, as well as a dozen pillows all covered with various colors of satin. The large room was softly carpeted, indirectly lighted, had original oil paintings on the walls, and classical music played from muted, excellent speakers.

The door across from Preacher opened and a tall, thin youth with sandy hair and hundreds of freckles came into the room.

"I told you we'd connect, I knew we could score!" the young man said, his right fist clenched and in the air.

Preacher frowned at him and pointed at a chair.

"How do you know that the Penetrator is deceased? You must realize the Penetrator is harder to kill than a water moccasin in a dark swamp at midnight. Jeffrey, punch up that tape."

A white man, about thirty, wearing a perfectly fitted suit with matching vest, and carefully styled hair, turned to a Betamax and snapped it on. A 48-inch TV screen nearby blinked into life and they watched a video tape of the 5:00 P.M. news film which showed a burning vehicle near the West Palm Beach airport. The announcer's voice came through abruptly.

"The car rental agency said a tall, dark man signed for the car, a new Granada, about an hour before it burst into flames in this ditch across from the airport. The driver's name was John Johnstone of Newark,

New Jersey, and he listed his occupation as salesman. Police say the car had been shot at least a dozen times, and witnesses say someone in a new Cadillac shot at the car, then backed up and threw two small bombs into the vehicle which blew it apart and set it on fire. No apparent reasons for the violence have been reported and, police said, since there was exploding ammunition inside the burning car, the fire was allowed to burn out before the last of the fire will be doused and the wreckage examined. They did not know for sure if the driver or any passengers were inside, but a search of the area immediately following the crash turned up no bodies nor anyone who had escaped from the blaze."

The fire burned on screen for a few seconds and faded out as the tape stopped.

"Well, Mr. Lee, now do you tell me that you scored? You are asking for the bonus I promised any man who eliminated the Penetrator?"

"Well, wow, Mr. Mann. I mean, no way he could get out of there. I nailed him with that ought-ought buck and the .44 magnum went through the sides of that car like butter, didn't you see. . . ."

Preacher held up his hand and the youth stopped.

"Mr. Lee, what I saw was one crafty honkey son-of-a-bitch who knew he was being hit and slid that Granada sideways, on purpose. Most of your slugs and all of the shotgun pellets went into the engine. He had the engine between him and your lousy little guns. You think you're dealing with some punk kid off the streets here? This man is an expert at combat warfare. He stayed alive in Vietnam for three or four years. He's blown more people away than you've spit on. This Penetrator dude was shooting the eyes out of

17

Viet Cong headmen and generals when you were still sucking at your mother's tit! I'll give you a hundred-to-one right now that you didn't kill the Penetrator and that there is no body in that wreck!"

Red Lee slipped a hundred-dollar bill out of his wallet and put it on the low table next to the big couch. "I have a hundred that says I got him. My shotgun just don't miss."

"Mr. Lee, it is a wager. Leave the bill there. Now, what I really wish you to explain is why you didn't take him out in the hangar. You had him one-to-one. You could have put a .45 to the back of his head before he knew it and blown his brains out. You could have been dead sure!"

Red Lee shook his head. "That would have ruined my cover at the hangar. A hit right there where I worked would be too easy to trace, to figure out. Even the stupid cops could have solved it. I had to get him outside, away. Anyhow, there's no sport in a surprise head shot like that. No sport at all."

Preacher Mann lifted his brows and tried to control his fury. "Little boy. With the Penetrator you take him out any way you can, anytime, and in anyplace. In the back, with his hands tied behind him and blindfolded if you can. Then under a ten-ton truck or into a cement mixer. You get him any way you can! And then you make certain and get him again. We don't play by a set of rules in this league."

Red frowned and shifted his position on the chair. "Okay, yeah, I see what you mean about the engine. Damn. I thought he was just going out of control. I thought. . . ."

Preacher dismissed him. "Next time, don't think, just shoot. Shoot the bastard and then you can think about it, or think how you're going to spend your money. Your hundred will be safe right there until we find out who it belongs to."

Red Lee nodded and headed for the door. Damn, but this was a creepy outfit to work for. He'd seen some of the muscle and power in Las Vegas, goons who could barely add, sharpies who didn't let anything get by them, old pros who could smell a trap or the heat a mile away, lowbrows, crude, uneducated action guys. This Preacher Mann was a weirdo, but he paid well. He wasn't a patsy, could outfight anybody Red had ever seen. But he had a master's degree from some college! He played classical records, for Christ's sake, for background music! The "advisers" around him wore three-hundred-dollar tailored suits and eighty-dollar shoes, and they all talked like some damned college professors. Red shook his head as he went out the door and down the hall to the day room where more classical music played, where they had a billiard table instead of a pool table, and four guys were playing bridge. Bridge! Christ, what kind of an outfit had he got mixed up with?

He'd been at the Pink Pussy until it got burned down that night, and he remembered that big guy, the Penetrator, very well. He had a photographic memory and he had known right away this was one face to remember. He had made drawings of that face and kept them. When this Penetrator became famous, Red had sent out letters to various businessmen and Mafia connections, explaining his contact with the bad man, and his memory for faces, and offering his services as lookout. He'd been at all sorts of places, worked for several different groups, but when the

Penetrator began using his own plane, Red knew he had him. He concentrated on the airport, the transient hangars. When he had it tied down that tightly, and when he found out the Penetrator now flew a Beech Duke, there was no way he could miss nailing the man eventually. He had been working on another plane when the Duke rolled in, but when he saw the profile and the face, even without the moustache, he knew he had his man. He phoned Preacher Mann for final instructions and after that, it was a piece of cake.

Red got coffee from a machine and began to wonder if they really did nail the Penetrator in that car. They hit it a dozen times with bullets and two loads of #00 buck, then used the fraggers. Naw—no way he could have gotten out of that rig alive, no way, even if the first broadside did miss. Still Red had one small wiggle of worry.

This Preacher Mann was one damned black creep, but he was color blind. He used the best man for the job, whether he was white, Cuban, Mexican, Arab, or black. They even had a Hawaiian who handled knife work.

Red had known about Preacher Mann for years. He began in Harlem running numbers and working up through the crime world. From numbers he went on to a young whore of his own when he was in high school, selling her by the hour to the high school jocks. By the time he got booted out of school he had three whores working for him, two black ones and a white. Three years later he was into pot and then heroin. His pushing business grew until he was a supplier and then a distributor. He had half the Harlem *H* trade when he pulled out and headed for Miami.

Those damn New York winters were too much for him.

But Preacher Mann had always admired smart people, and he went back to night school when he was eighteen to get his high school diploma and then signed up at City College in New York, and eventually got a degree in history and Eastern European art.

Even when he moved to Florida he hung onto his Harlem trade, and there in West Palm Beach he had gone legitimate. He owned the building he sat in, had a dozen other functioning businesses, and ran tons of pot and all the *H* he could get from Mexico. It was Mexican Brown now, but the hypes didn't care.

He picked up his "preacher" nickname in Harlem when he went wild over vegetarian food. He kept preaching about vegetarian eating so much he got tagged with the preacher label and it stuck. Now, after almost ten years of operation in this end of Florida, he had sewn up his city and state protection. He was literally untouchable by any law enforcement arm in the state. The Preacher didn't flaunt it, but if one of his men was charged with a crime, he was bailed out quickly, and always by a different, highly legitimate criminal lawyer. Trials were delayed and delayed and many times thrown out of court for lack of witnesses or evidence.

Lately Red heard the big man had gone into the international trade, working with intelligence people, offering to get any information about defense, arms, or missiles from any country for any other country. He had a lot of inquiries and was working to get some solid contracts.

Red knew little about the "Island Operation." That was the latest, and the only thing he had heard about it was that the big man had spent over two million dollars putting in some kind of an installation there, spending money for machinery, engineers and construction, but nobody seemed to know anything about it. Every time he asked questions he was told he had no need to know about it, so not to ask. Need to know? Christ, that was army talk. This wasn't the damn army!

One project Preacher Mann made no secret of: girls. Although the big man did not smoke, drink, eat meat, or use drugs, he did have one vice—girls. He went through dozens of them. The business side was officially known as an executive outcall escort service. There was almost no special girl the Preacher couldn't furnish if the customer would pay enough. He could come up with a gymnast, tight ropewalker, opera singer, a symphony violinist, tennis pro, TV or motion picture star, and usually in any color or shape, size or race.

Right now Red Lee didn't know what kind he wanted, but he certainly was going to try something different from the Preacher's stock of delicacies. He went up to the eleventh floor and talked to the manager, Monique. She showed him her "on-call" chart and told him to take his pick. He decided on the little gymnast and told Monique to send her to his pad on the other side of town in an hour. By then he should know what the cops had found in that goddamned rented Granada, and it would be time to celebrate.

## Chapter 3

## SOFT HIT—RECON

After Mark registered at the Sea Breeze Motel and had a long, hot shower, he walked along the beach front to a closed telephone booth, dialed the police, and asked for the criminal investigation department.

"This is C.I.D.," a bored female voice said.

"Hi there, sugar, is this Betty?"

"No, she doesn't work here."

"Well, you'll do just fine, sugar. Got a plate I need checked out—wants, warrants and registration. It's Frank, Albert, Zero, Nine, Five, One. Push that into your magic machine there, honey."

"Yes. You'll wait?"

"Right on, sugar. I don't think I've seen you down there, you new? What's your name?"

"I don't have a name, just a number, 546-31-7910, Sugar."

"Come on, don't put me down. I'm just a lonely cop trying to maintain my sanity."

"Sure, sugar, sure you are. On that plate, no wants

or warrants. A 1978 Cadillac, blue, four door. Registered to Babco Leasing. Anything else, sugar?"

"Nope, sweetheart, that does it. I'm gonna find out who you are yet, you wait and see."

"I'll wait."

Mark hung up grinning, and checked out Babco Leasing in the phone book: 6915 Harland Street. So far, so good. Now he was ready for that early dinner and then he would go prospecting.

Mark hurried back to the Sea Breeze and went up to his fourth-floor ocean-view room and checked in his weapons case. There it was, a neat duplicate set of his data file on Preacher Mann that the professor had built for him. The originals had burned up in the Granada fire. He took the package and sat down in a chair and flipped the TV on to catch the local news. The top story was about the attack on his Granada. They even had footage of the car burning in the ditch, with the cops trying to keep the people back.

Mark was grateful the Granada had protected him so well, and was glad he was in one piece so he could crawl out as fast as he did. Those grenades would have been right in his lap if he waited even half a minute. That would have been the end of the Penetrator.

Mark called room service and ordered a blood-rare steak, making sure the chef would sear it on both sides. He also ordered a quart of milk.

Mark laid out on the bed all of his material on Preacher Mann. He had been over it three times lately but he looked at it all again. There had been a spate of bad publicity about Preacher Mann two years ago, but since that time very little showed in the public prints. There was more action on the police teletype. Preacher was tied into the Harlem drug scene, but there was not enough evidence to prosecute. He also was loosely associated with three men in the Miami area who had fatal accidents, but again, there was not enough evidence to get an indictment. Once he was charged by the Florida state police commission with being an active member of organized crime, but the accusations were never made again, and never were acted upon.

The fact remained that Preacher Mann had never been arrested for anything in the state of Florida, not even overtime parking.

His activities centered in the West Palm Beach area, but he was invisible, handling his operations through more than a dozen different legitimate businesses in diversified fields. He bought up a going firm, a profit making concern, and put in his man as a top level watchdog, but let the company function as before. Soon he began adding departments that were run by the newcomers, yet the whole thing was under the main firm's umbrella. No one disputed the ridiculously high profit picture of the new enterprises, especially top men who got increased salaries.

When the steak came Mark thanked the waiter. When he cut into the meat, blood seeped out, and Mark grinned. Just the way he liked it and David Red Eagle would have approved. He drank the milk as he ate the rare steak and went over the last of the details they had about Preacher Mann. It wasn't enough. He didn't have a real starting place. That's what worried him.

There was a chance that the attempted hit this afternoon had been on orders of Preacher Mann. If so, his inspection of Babco should give him a lead in that direction. That was his next project.

He bundled up the material about the Preacher and put it all in his arms suitcase, then opened the other piece of luggage and shook out a new sport jacket.

Florida wasn't the place for sport jackets this time of year, but it had a special purpose. He checked it closely but to him it looked like any other sport jacket. The weave did seem rather tight and a little harder than he liked.

The fabric was called "Resistweve," and came out of California where a small firm had just completed a new process. This sport jacket would resist a .38 slug or anything smaller at nearly point blank range if the bullet hit at other than an eighty-eight to ninety-two degree angle against a flat surface. A perpendicular shot would penetrate the fabric, but with much less power than normal and probably would slow the bullet so it couldn't penetrate a body more than an inch at the most.

A man in Newport Beach had worked out the mechanics of it and this was the first known coat of its kind. The inventor began with a special fabric woven of tough Kevlar synthetic fiber and metallic threads. The ultra-thin weave was then heat bonded together into three thicknesses, with the heavier vertical threads in each layer crossing each other at ninety degrees, much like the grain does in three-ply plywood. Then two of these triple fabric packs were put together with a newly developed flexible fabric adhesive which would stretch a little and give, but then snap back, and at the same time had the most amazing anti-penetration properties. The entire sandwich of six plies when finished was slightly thicker than the material in a fine Pendleton shirt, and this Resistweve fabric was then tripled in thickness for making the jacket.

The new Resistweve came in a wide variety of colors and patterns, but only the two weights, one for shirts and pants, the heavier stuff for jackets. The material looked and felt much like a heavy pair of army-issue wool pants, Mark thought. He slipped into the pants, put on the shirt and tucked the tails in, then put on the jacket, leaving the shirt collar open and on the outside in a casual style. He found enough room built in under the left arm, as he had instructed, for his light-weight leather shoulder holster, and slid in his .22 High Standard automatic.

Mark took out a silent tranquilizer gun, Ava, which shot sleep darts, powered by $CO_2$ cartridges. The loads could be changed from tranquilizer to deadly curarine poison tips for a silent killing weapon. The darts were good for twenty yards with acceptable accuracy. Mark used it mainly for going past innocents who needed to be put down and usually were armed, but did not need to be killed. Ava slid into a clip-on belt holster under his jacket.

The Penetrator strapped on his wrist knife in its sleek sheath that tied on his forearm. The stilleto could be dislodged and dropped into his hand with a sudden twist-flexing of his wrist. In his pocket Mark carried a hideout gun, one of his pair of potent little .22 magnum derringers.

The Penetrator didn't take any of the other small surprises from his arm suitcase. He carefully locked it and put it in the closet so some enterprising maid didn't discover his illegal hardware.

Mark closed his door, locked it, and went down to

his Dodge Monaco and drove toward the Babco Leasing company on Harland Street.

The building was three stories tall, and proved to be a rental firm that didn't know when to stop. It spread out into a yard that contained dozens of small construction and do-it-yourself rigs from skip loaders to small cranes. On the first and second floors they had other rental equipment from hospital beds to game and party supplies including rental fine crystal for a fancy dinner. They also leased cars and trucks.

Mark drove to the rear of the place, parked, and watched for any guard activity. He spotted a middle-aged man, with ex-cop stenciled all over him, who made a key-lock stop near the back gate to prove to some sensitive computer watchdog brain that he actually had made his rounds at the gate. Then the rent-a-cop vanished.

The Penetrator grinned. Like any good ex-cop he would hit every key-in station on time, and probably do little else. Mark should have at least an hour before the guard came back that way. The Penetrator went over the chain link fence easily, stepping over the barbed wire on the top and dropping into the complex. He ran for the side door where the guard had vanished, knowing it would be locked. The lock was harder than Mark guessed; it took him more than a minute to pick it open, then he slid inside, and heard no alarms or angry voices. He looked around and found himself on the ground floor of the main building with a stairway that led upward. Mark always liked to start at the top and work down, then there should be fewer surprises. He started up the steps quietly and was halfway, when the guard stepped out at the top.

"Hold it right there, friend. This is the end of the line for you."

Mark looked at the guard, and saw that he was not sleepy-eyed or slow; rather he was alert, and his .38 was aimed precisely at Mark's heart, his knees were slightly bent, his feet, set apart. The man had combat and hand to hand fighting experience, Mark could tell. So he would play it cool.

"There you are. I've been looking for you. That rear gate is unlocked, did you know that? Mr. Johnson is going to be mad as hell when he finds out."

"Sure he is. And of course you've been looking for me. That's why you parked your Dodge Monaco a block from the back gate and watched me make my rounds. That's why you climbed over the fence and followed me into this building by picking the door lock. Sure, you've been looking all over the plant for me. Now, back down the steps one at a time, and don't make any funny moves. I can use this thirty-eight."

Mark moved slowly as directed and at once saw the guard's mistake. There was no door at the bottom of the steps, but there was a partition to his left. One surging jump there and he'd be out of the man's sight, and the gun's power.

"Don't move toward either side, stay right in the middle of the steps, friend. You're not going anywhere."

Mark stepped down two more steps, wishing he could make a fast draw with Ava. This guard was legitimate, a sheep, not one of the goats he could eliminate. He had to separate the sheep from the goats. But what did he do next?

Mark saw the last step coming and watched the

other man's eyes. He had moved with Mark, by feel, going down each step, wanting to look down to check his footing but not daring. Mark guessed that sooner or later the guard's glance would drop to be sure where the next step was and when it did. . . .

The man's glance shifted downward to the steps for the flash of an eye-blink, but it was long enough for Mark to lunge sideways. The .38 roared in the stairwell and Mark knew he would be shot. The slug angled at him, the ex-cop shooting for the biggest body mass and leading his chest just enough. Mark almost made it, then the .38 slug struck his sport jacket over his left ribs at a forty-five-degree angle.

Mark yelped at the impact but his momentum carried him beyond the side of the stairway at the bottom of the steps and out of sight. He felt of his chest and knew he had been hurt, but he didn't know how badly. His ribs ached like they had been hit with a hammer; stabbing pains darted through his chest and brain, but even as they pelted him, he had hit the floor, completing his dive, rolled and jumped up, pulling Ava from her nest. He stepped back to the edge of the stairs and sent a sleep dart into the surprised guard as he came down the steps cautiously. The guard was so startled to see Mark standing that he didn't even try a second shot.

The dart penetrated the man's blue uniform shirt and jolted the M-99 and sodium pentothal into his chest. Instantaneously his chest and arms began to cramp from the special ingredient in the mixture and the guard slumped to the steps and rolled toward Mark, who caught him. Ten seconds after the dart entered his body, the guard's muscle spasms ceased and he was tranquilized from the powerful drugs. He would wake up in fifteen to twenty minutes with a slight headache. Mark pushed the guard against the wall and looked down at his own chest where he had been shot.

The outside of the fabric showed a bruise, a slight stretching, but there was no difference at all inside the fabric. The bullet had not penetrated! His shirt was intact and so was his chest. Only his ribs hurt and he guessed he might have a bruised rib or two. He'd exchange that for being alive. The damn fabric did work; the Resistweve had passed its first test.

He rubbed his chest and began a hurried examination of the building. For ten minutes he prowled offices, storerooms, warehouses and work areas. He discovered nothing unusual. Then on the third floor addition in back, he found what he wanted, a locked room at the very top of the complex. He opened the door easily and inside saw a sophisticated communications room. It had some highly technical gear, including short-wave transmitters that could pick up and send to any major city in the world. There was printout equipment from some kind of wire service, and CW sets for sending and receiving code on continuous radio waves and that unit also had a printout. Mark was sure some of the equipment would broadcast messages designed to bounce off satellites. Two tables had consoles with mike stands and some kind of readout screens in front of them. Mark wondered why no one was working. It must be an around-the-clock operation. Certainly something like this was not needed by a rental store.

On a desk near some of the equipment he found the carbon copy of a repair order from Atlantic Electronics. It listed six calls to make for regular electronic maintenance and repair on a contract with Babco. This address was one of them, and there were five other locations listed. All charges were to go to Babco. Mark took the list and retraced his steps to the hallway where he had left the snoozing guard. He was still out. He'd be coming around soon. Mark put a two-and-one-half-inch chipped blue flint arrowhead in the guard's hand. The man would find it when he woke up, groggy and angry. This was one job where Mark thought a little newspaper publicity might be helpful. Right now he wanted to let whoever had tried to waste him know for sure that the hit hadn't worked. That should bring some action, and the assassins out of the woodwork in a rush!

## Chapter 4

## DEATHLY DOUBLE DOORWAY

Mark had visited the first four firms listed on the electronics repair order and found absolutely nothing suspicious. All were small, harmless, and with no potential for violence. He had no idea how they tied in with his suspicions concerning the complex communications set up at Babco. All that wattage certainly was not for any legitimate business purpose. The other firms he checked included a small truck line, a small marine construction outfit, and a fleet of six fishing boats. All had radios.

That made for a lot of diversification, but some corporations liked to spread out the risks that way. Mark filed it all away in his memory for possible later call up, and drove to the last business on the list, Dunsmuir Warehouse Company. That's all it was, a warehouse. The Penetrator could see nothing inside, and just the firm's name on a small unlighted sign outside. It gave him an uneasy feeling. Why so airtight? Why so anonymous? He drove around the half-block structure, came back and parked in front of it. The time was 2:00 A.M. and he saw nothing except a night light beside a man-sized front door. The loading docks with their truck roll-up doors were all silent and dark.

On a chance there was a watchman, he parked and went up to the lighted door and pushed the night buzzer. He could hear a bell ring far away. Mark hit the button a second time and soon a small microphone over the door came to life.

"Yeah, whadda ya want?"

"I have a special air shipment, a package. The pilot told me it was crew special and I should deliver it to this address at any time of the day or night and get it signed for. Come on, man, open up, I got to get home and get some damned sleep."

"We don't take packages here."

"You'll take this one or I'll deliver it to the cops. The pilot said he brought in something special from Mexico City, around customs, I'd bet sure as hell. Now, come on, man. I just got a job to do, so take the goddamned package and sign my slip so I can get away from here and you can get back to sleep."

Mark heard a grumble over the intercom, then the bolt was thrown and the door eased open. As soon as he saw the man, the Penetrator fired a sleep dart into him, and he crumpled inside. Mark slid into the warehouse and pushed the twitching guard away so he could close the door. Then he studied the man in the faint beams of the distant night light. First he stripped the old .45 from the hanging holster, removed the clip and threw it down the aisle. It clattered loudly in the quiet place.

"Any problems, Will?" a voice asked from deeper into the warehouse.

34

Mark stepped back out of the light and into the dark shadows next to some large wooden crates. Thirty seconds passed.

"Well, goddamnit, Will, if you opened that door again for some stumble bum, it's gonna be your ass this time. I warned you. Will?"

The Penetrator heard the steps come quietly, but the man didn't blunder into the lighted area. He was smart. He must have looked it over first and seen Will flat on his back by the door.

"Whoever the hell you are, mister, you're a dead man. Nobody comes in here and coldcocks our guard. You're in big trouble and there's no way out except that little door. So you just get yourself ready to die!"

Mark hadn't moved, hovering in the shadows down one aisle. The boxes were cardboard with wooden frames, stacked eight feet high along here and the voice was somewhere beyond the end of the boxes. Mark took the guard's .45 and tossed it toward the voice. Two quick shots blazed in the darkness of the big warehouse, the booming sounds fading off into its far reaches.

When the area quieted Mark could hear nothing but his own soft breathing. He slowed his heart rate and listened for the other man's presence. There was something—movement—breathing on top of the crates. Up there. The Penetrator moved silently away from the door until he could see the outline of the top of the boxes in the glow of the far off light. He waited.

First a hand came over the side, gripping the wood, then another hand appeared and a head pushed over between them, the man evidently staring into the blackness below him. Mark bent low, then sprang upward, grabbed the head and twisted it out and downward. A surprised gurgling scream came from the other guard's throat and two shots sounded in a reflex action before Mark hauled him down and slammed him into the cement warehouse floor. The victim groaned and rolled over, then the gun blazed twice more, and shots going wild. Mark returned the fire in an automatic combat reflex, the dart gun jolting twice in his hand. There was just enough light to see the darts hit the young man's arm and chest. He was unconscious in ten seconds. Mark tied him securely.

Mark waited a few moments to see if there was anyone else in the big building. He had no doubts that the man with the quick trigger was one of the goats. His kind always shot first and asked questions second. When the silence persisted in the warehouse, the Penetrator checked the body, then dragged it back out of the aisle away from the door and out of sight of the first tranquilized guard.

Mark made a quick inspection of the warehouse. Most of it was empty. One section held small boxes, another had the huge boxes with wooden crating. These were marked "Refrigeration Specialists." To one side he saw a dozen more boxes that had pictures on the outside showing something that looked a little like a casket, but it also looked like the astronaut's space seats. The Penetrator didn't know what they were or why they were worth shooting at people for, like the young guard had. He went back to the door and watched the older man come out of the tranquilizer.

The guard's eyes rolled, his hands jerked, then his feet made strange motions and at last his hands formed into fists and his eyes seemed to come into focus. The howl of pain tumbled from his throat as the man touched his head tenderly.

"Damn! Goddamn it. What'n hell was that? Who was the son-of-a-bitch who hit me from behind?"

He rolled over and stared at Mark who squatted nearby, his High Standard .22 aimed at the man's chest.

"Take it easy, now, and you'll live to see tomorrow," the Penetrator said. "What's your name?"

"Lubowski, Will Lubowski."

"Who do you work for?"

"Dunsmuir Warehousing."

"As a night guard?"

"Yeah, my tenth year. Nobody ever slipped up behind me that way before. How'n hell you do that?"

"Secret. Who owns Dunsmuir Warehousing?"

"Mr. Dunsmuir? How the hell should I know?"

"Ever heard of Babco?"

"Sure, leasing outfit. We have some of their trucks in here sometimes, so what?"

"They also own Dunsmuir Warehousing, and half a dozen other firms. Do you have an emergency trouble number?"

"Naw, nothing goes wrong."

"You sure? What about the Babco Leasing rigs? Any special precautions when their stuff is in here?"

"Why should there be? Naw. Just that once. Some Mr. Big Shot came and wanted to stay with the rigs all night, but he got tired and stiff and said I should call him if anybody so much as rang the night bell. I mean he was spooky, and scared. Gave me a number, so I write it down in my book."

"Tell me the number?"

"Hell, no."

37

Mark took a packet out of his shirt pocket and opened it. He showed the guard the two syringes and the six vials of fluid. Four of the tubes had different color codes on them.

"You ever been drugged, Lubowski? Ever had a needle pushed into your arm, and soon you didn't know what you were saying, or who you were, and you'd tell the truth about anything you were asked?"

"Hey, stay away from me with that shit!"

"This red one, Lubowski. It's the quick death kind. I put that into your veins and you've got about seven minutes of the worst pain you have ever imagined before you die. Would you like me to demonstrate?"

"No," Lubowski said, sweat popping out on his forehead, his arms folding and unfolding. He kept looking at the gun that lay near Mark's side.

"Lubowski, I could use this yellow tipped one. It's filled with just enough sodium pentothal to make you sing like a canary, to spill your guts in a big pile."

"Now, look. . . ."

"Do you owe this much to your employer, Lubowski?"

He shook his head.

"So give me that number this nervous guy asked you to call if anything went wrong."

The guard took out a small plastic notebook and leafed through the pages.

"Here it is, right here. Almost six months ago." He read off the phone number and Mark memorized it.

"Thanks, Will. Now, if you don't mind, I'm going to have to tie you up. Your relief should be here at about seven in the morning and untie you. Don't worry about your buddy. He can't help you. You tell your boss exactly what happened in the morning, understand?"

The Penetrator took a small roll of twenty pound monofilament fishing line from his pocket and tied the guard's feet together. Then he told Lubowski to put his hands behind his back and Mark tied them.

When Mark laid the blue flint arrowhead beside the watchman he looked up in surprise.

"Hey, that looks like a real one. Is it?"

"Yes."

"Can I have it?"

"It mean anything to you, Will?"

"Nope, but my grandchild would like it."

"Good, after you show it to your boss, tell him I want you to keep it for the kid."

Mark smiled as he left the building, making sure that the small door latched and locked behind him. It wouldn't hurt to check out the phone company information people, and maybe he could imitate a real Florida cop on the beat. He drove a half mile to an unlit telephone booth and dialed the operator.

"This is police business. I'd like to speak to your supervisor, please," he told the first voice.

A moment later a new voice came on the line.

"Ma'am, I'm Detective Harbinson. I don't have time to go through channels for this, but I have a phone number and my partner is there and in trouble and I need the address just as quick as I can get it." He read her the phone number.

"This is all quite irregular," she said.

"I know. I'm Detective Sergeant Harbinson. Edwin L., Badge #456, West Palm Beach PD. I need that address and this is the only way I can get it. My partner may be bleeding to death right now, can't you rush it!"

"All right, I'll route you through, but you fill out the paper work in the morning."

Two minutes later he had the address, 1313 Broadway. It sounded like it was right downtown. He got out of the phone booth and hoped there wasn't a real Detective Harbinson on the local cop force. If there was, he'd have some answers to give tomorrow.

The Penetrator drove to the address and whistled. It was the Florida Home Savings and Loan building, with eleven stories, and a half-block square. Surely he got the wrong number from the guard or the operator. He checked his memory circuits and was sure of the digits. Mark circled the structure and found only the one big number on Broadway. This was it.

He eased the Monaco to the curb across the street and studied the big place. Besides the Savings and Loan, there were other ground floor retail outlets, and probably hundreds of offices on the other ten floors. Did Babco own all this, too, or did this one own Babco? Maybe he had been going at it backward. Perhaps Babco was only one of the chain, one of the legalized business firms they knew Preacher Mann had in this city.

The Penetrator looked up at the top floors; everything was dark. Not a light showed and why should it at almost 3:00 A.M.? He was going to have to get back to his motel and catch a few hours of sleep before he barged into this place tomorrow to check it out.

It was a hot, muggy Florida night, and Mark had been driving with both the front windows down. He took one last look at the high rise, then growled in frustration and reached to turn the ignition key.

"Don't touch it, buddy," a voice said from the passenger's side window. The Penetrator looked over at the black hole of a .45 automatic aimed precisely at his heart.

## Chapter 5

## BROADWAY SHOTGUN WELCOME

"Be most cautious, sir, in your movements," the voice outside the passenger side window said. "I would appreciate it if you would get out of the car and come with me."

"Why the hell should I?"

"Because I have this gun trained on you, sir."

"What for? It's against the law to park on the street now? When the hell they pass that law?"

"We have been watching you drive around the building, then you sat and stared at it and checked the building number. It's after 3:00 A.M., sir, and that makes you highly suspicious. You also resemble the description of a man we're looking for. If you are not armed and no danger to our people you will be released."

"Big deal. You kidnap me and talk to me like you're some damned professor. I guess you won't mind if I unfasten my seat belt. I always like to use the belts—good protection. This town has some nutty drivers.

One ran me off the road yesterday. I'm going to reach over and unbuckle my seat belt now, so don't get an itchy trigger finger. I'm curious about who thinks they own the goddamn streets in this hick town."

As he talked, Mark reached slowly toward his seat belt, twist flexing his right wrist to release the knife on his forearm. The blade slid down point first and he let it come, covering it with his wrist and hand. As he struggled with the seat belt clasp, he looked up in frustration.

"Hey, buddy, you know how this one works? These damn rental cars all have different kinds of belt releases."

As Mark said it, the stiletto blade slid past his fingers and he caught the handle. In a movement so fast it caught the man outside completely by surprise, Mark lunged sideways across the seat and slashed the wrist that held the .45 which had edged inside the car window.

The gunman screamed and his reflex action triggered a shot that missed Mark; then he dropped the .45. The explosion of the automatic inside the car was eardrum splitting, but Mark knew the slug had missed him and the gun was on the floor of the car.

He ducked under the windows searching for the big gun just as a load of buckshot hit a rear tire, dropping the Monaco to its rim.

The Penetrator knew there was a backup man now, so he pushed the passenger side door open a foot, drawing handgun fire, then he grabbed the dropped automatic, leaped from the driver's side of the car and darted along a row of rigs parked at the curb ahead of him. He heard two shots behind him. The rear window of the car he was passing shattered as a bullet blasted through it. Mark dodged in and out between the cars for a half block to the corner where a red light glowed.

A Datsun sedan swept up to the light and stopped a dozen feet ahead of him. Mark ran for the car, jerked the door open on the passenger's side and leaped inside.

"Move it!" he shouted. He saw the driver was a young woman. "Drive, go through the damn light! I've got two killers chasing me with guns. Drive, now!"

She looked at him, her face a shocked white, but she stepped on the accelerator, gunning them through the deserted intersection and down the block.

"Turn left next block," he commanded. She did.

At the next corner they turned right and he kept them twisting through the street but always away from the big building on Broadway. He hadn't looked at her yet—he was watching behind. So far he had seen no pursuit of any kind. Nearly a mile from 1313 Broadway, he knew they were in the clear.

"Turn into that next alley to the left, go through to the far end and stop."

When she was there he told her to turn off the lights but to leave the engine running.

He settled back now and studied her carefully.

"I'm sorry about this, young lady. I had no other options. There were two hoodlums back there trying to punch holes in my skin with .45 automatics."

She was trembling.

"What's your name?"

"Kristi."

"Look, Kristi, you can relax now. I'm terribly sorry, I didn't mean to frighten you, and I'm not going to rob you or hurt you. I'll get out right now and let you go on wherever you were going if you want me to. It's just that when a man's life is in the balance, he sometimes inconveniences others to save himself."

He looked at her in the pale light and saw that she was young, not over twenty-two, with long brown hair in a Farrah Fawcett set. Her eyes were brown, too, he guessed and wide set over a slender nose and a small mouth with full, sensuous lips.

She still hadn't said anything but her name. She shivered again and sat there with her hands in her lap, staring straight ahead. At last she gave a long sigh.

"My horoscope said this was going to be a bad day, but I didn't expect anything like this."

Her voice was soft, lyrical with a gentle rhythm that he couldn't tie down to a locality. She turned to look at him now.

"You are a very insistent person, a Virgo, I'd bet. I don't know why I'm chattering away like this. Do you think I might be a little nervous? Scared spitless is more nearly the truth. I just don't know if I can handle something like this. Now if you were six years old, had hurt your knee, had a runny nose or couldn't climb the noddle-knocker pole, I'd know exactly what to do."

"School teacher?" he asked.

"Yes. So tomorrow I tell the kids to write an essay on 'The first time I was kidnapped,' Oh, wow! I am going off the deep end. These kids are kindergarten and can't even write yet."

He watched her relax a little. The shivering stopped; she could look at him now without her eyes going narrow and frightened.

46

"Look, could I make this up to you? You saved my life back there. How about dinner or a drink or a snack somewhere?"

"At three-thirty in the morning?"

"Yeah, that does sound a little strange, doesn't it?"

"Are they still chasing you? Do they know where you live? Will they find you again?"

"Probably, to all three."

"Well, then we should go to my apartment and have some coffee and talk until the sun comes up." She frowned. "I'm not offering to share my bed with you, but there's a big, soft chair and a couch that you can take a nap on if you want to."

She turned and lifted her carefully fashioned brows. "I don't even know your name."

"Doug."

"A good, solid, rugged name. Are you a Virgo?"

"I really don't know."

"Not a fan, I see. Well, what's your decision? Do you want to share a cup of coffee with an old maid school teacher? That's what my wanting-to-be-a-grandmother, mother, calls me."

"Yes, I'd like that cup of coffee."

They made a detour on the way to her apartment. Whoever the gunmen were, they now had his Monaco and could trace the rental slip and get the name he used to rent it, then check motels quickly. He had to clear out of the Sea Breeze fast. Mark directed her to the back of the parking lot and told her to keep her windows rolled up and doors locked. He vanished into the darkness, cleaned out his room and was back in five minutes. She jumped when he knocked on the car door, then let him in quietly.

Mark had her drive out of the parking lot and go

47

two blocks before he let her turn on her lights. No sense in getting her mixed up in any of this.

Her apartment was back from the beach not too far away, and she had redecorated it when she took it over a year ago. It was bright and youthful, cheery and filled with early Goodwill and later second-hand store furniture, most of which had been expertly refinished, stained, varnished or painted. It was three rooms and a bath. She even showed him her prize wrought-iron bed.

"I decided just to paint this one," she said, "it seems to fit in well." When the tour was over, she went to the kitchen and made coffee as they talked.

"Somebody really was trying to kill you?"

"Trying as hard as they could."

She took a deep breath. "And did you kill any of them?" Her eyes were wide. This was probably the first time she had ever talked to anyone who had just been shot at.

"I only gave one a little slice on the wrist so he'd drop his gun."

She sipped her coffee, her brown eyes wide, hair falling over her ears, face somber, impressed.

"Could I see your gun?"

He showed her Ava, explaining that it was a tranquilizer dart gun.

"But there's a lag from the time the dart hits a person and when he goes unconscious. Isn't that why police don't use this kind of a weapon?"

He laughed.

"Kristi, I'm surprise. Most people don't understand about tranquilizing that well. Why do you?"

"I started school as a criminology major. I did a paper on alternate weapons for law officers. There

48

wasn't anything that would work then. Any good gunman can get off two or three shots a second, and in ten seconds he could empty his gun twice over after he was darted and before he passed out."

Mark explained the muscle spasming agent they used that functioned almost simultaneously with injection.

She watched him over the top of her coffee cup and he had the impression that she was still hiding behind it. "Then, Doug, you're one of the good guys, and those others back there were the bad guys?"

"That's a good way to put it. Why not?" He put the dart gun away. "Why did you switch to education from criminology?"

"Chicken."

They both laughed.

"Do you want some toast, some jam, orange juice? I don't have any breakfast rolls, and it is almost time for breakfast." She lifted her eyes to heaven for help. "Now I'm sounding so damn domestic it's pathetic. Can't I ever act just right? Cool but sophisticated and at the same time, charming?" She shook her head. "I guess I'm still scared, or maybe scared again." Kristi stood and leaned on the back of the chair staring at him. "I'm not used to having anyone here, let alone a handsome and exciting man like you. Which is my parting soliloquy. If I don't get at least three hours of sleep, I'll be an impossibly nasty old nag tomorrow with the small ones. Now, you can have the rest of the place, just as soon as I brush my teeth. I've got to get some sleep." She went into the bathroom and closed the door.

Mark began evaluating his situation. He didn't have

any wheels, his second I.D. name was blown, and he was sleeping on a couch.

At least he had one small lead on the trouble, the big Florida Home Savings building. That was a start. How many rooms in there had telephones? But he had a direct number which might cut out switchboards, or would it?

He took off his sport jacket and hung it on a chair, then slipped off his shoes and was unbuttoning the Resistweve shirt when Kristi came from the bathroom.

"I've got a new tooth. . . ." She stopped and looked at him. "You're the first man who has ever taken off his shirt in my apartment. I don't know if that's a confession or if I'm bragging." She tossed him a slim plastic case. "Here's a new toothbrush if you want one." She walked to the bathroom door and turned, smiling.

"Doug, I'm sure you're very adult and sophisticated about these things, but I'm not. I guess I'm still just a little bit scared. I trust you and I like you. I guess that's why I let you come here and kind of hide out. But I am not one of those wildly liberated women types who goes to bed with a man every other night just to prove how free she is." Kristi laughed nervously. "I don't know why I thought I had to say that. Maybe to reassure myself. Is that possible? My psychology 201 grades were never very good."

She put her hands on the door, and Mark stayed where he was by the couch.

"Well, good night. Sleep well."

"Kristi, will it be all right if I leave my suitcase here? I might be gone when you get up this morning. Right now I don't have a place to roost."

"Oh, sure, fine. Leave them if you want. And if you come back tomorrow for dinner, I'll unfreeze something. I'm not the world's greatest cook, but we'll have something."

"Thanks, I'll try to be here." He watched her go into the bedroom and he realized that she was more than attractive. She was young and vulnerable, interesting and exciting, the kind of girl that can grow on you so fast you might not want to let go.

Mark shook his head and stretched out on the couch. This wasn't in the script, not at all. Tomorrow he'd put his suitcases in a bus depot locker or get a motel room somewhere and he'd never see Kristi again. He remembered too many innocents who had been hurt just because they knew him or tried to help.

That would simply not be permitted to happen again.

## Chapter 6

## TABLER UNDER THE GUN

Joanna Tabler had arrived in West Palm Beach late the previous night and went straight to her hotel, the Royal, where she fell into bed so exhausted that she didn't even watch the late news show on TV at eleven, so she missed hearing about the rented car that had blown up and burned that afternoon.

The next morning her alarm failed to wake her at 7:30 A.M. Joanna hadn't perfected her mental alarm, and her windup clock simply did not do the job. She usually didn't leave a call with the room clerk; that was one element of failure she tried to go around. When she woke at 8:30, she knew she would have to rush to make her ten o'clock appointment downtown. A fast shower and then careful makeup work and dressing left only ten minutes for a quick breakfast snack she had sent to her room. She saw the newspaper headlines in the racks as she hurried for a taxi, something about a car burning up near the airport. But she did not read the story, so she didn't discover in the last paragraph a report by police that the strangest item they found in one bullet-riddled aluminum suitcase was a group of twenty-five blue flint, chipped arrowheads. If she had seen it she would have known immediately that Mark Hardin was in town, that the Penetrator was here, and she would have tried to find him.

Joanna Tabler did not look like an operative for the Justice Department. At twenty-eight she still had her model's figure of 36-24-37, and her platinum blonde hair, neither long nor short, always looked as though she had just stepped out of the hair dresser's. She worked under cover from Diogenes Investigations in New York City, where she ran a plush office high in a tower with expensive surroundings and a secretary, as well as a telephone line to her boss, Dan Griggs in Washington D.C.

Joanna wasn't just attractive or pretty, she was beautiful, with striking hazel eyes, a finely chiseled nose and cheekbones that were just a little high to lend a note of mystery about her ancestry. She carried a J-6 agent rating, only two steps from the top, and a .38 revolver in her purse.

When she got out of the cab she looked up at the address to be sure, 1313 Broadway, double lucky. Joanna checked her watch, saw that she was already two minutes late, so hurried through the big doors to the elevator and got off on the ninth floor. Three years ago she had done the first work on this case, then a year ago it came alive, and now she was responding to a request for an infiltration into the firm if possible. She had made an appointment the day before to talk about a job. She direct dialed it from New York, and there was no way they could tell it was not

54

a local call. She was to contact a Mr. Bompensiero at 10:00 A.M. in room 926.

Joanna wore cool separates, pure white flared pants and a short buttoned jacket over a light blue cowl-neck cotton top. She wanted to look cool, efficient and not too casual. The light blue purse she carried had the rest of her gear, and her .38 revolver.

The cover name of Babco Leasing showed on the door. Joanna put on her best camera-ready smile and walked in. The reception room was big, and softly stylish, underplayed just enough so you could feel the expense of the decor and furnishings. The double-thick rug gave her a clue. She kept her smile on for the expensively dressed, high-fashion-type model receptionist, who stared at Joanna like she was a country bumpkin who had stumbled through the wrong door.

"Miss, would you tell Mr. Bompensiero that I'm here? I have an appointment for 10:05."

The receptionist glanced at the clock on the wall, saw it showing exactly 10:05, and picked up a phone. Although Joanna stood less than four feet from the girl, she could not hear the words spoken. A moment later the stately, thin girl behind the desk nodded, unsmiling, at Joanna.

"See his secretary, please, third door on your right along that corridor." The receptionist continued a look of either scorn or pity, Joanna wasn't sure which. She decided to play it broad.

"Thanks, honey. I like your dress," then she was gone down the corridor counting doors. Joanna walked in at the third one which had the Bompensiero name on it.

This woman was older, about forty, her chic several

55

shades less expensive and less expert, and she could probably even type. Her smile looked human and there were a few crinkle lines at the corners of her eyes.

"Hello, I have an appointment with Mr. Bompensiero. I hope I'm not late."

The woman looked uncertain for just a moment, then brightened. "Oh, yes, gracious, you're Melody Martin, you were the 10:00. I'd nearly forgotten. Mr. Bompensiero is busy right now, dear, but I'll let him know that you're here."

She was still sitting at her desk and now flipped a switch, then typed on a small keyboard.

"Can I get you some coffee?" the secretary asked.

"Oh, no thanks, I'll just wait. What a lot of plants you have here. You must have a real green thumb."

The woman's smile flowered. "Yes, I do have a few plants, but I keep most of them at home. That diffenbachia is just growing like a weed this year. If you want any Creeping Charlie, I have eight varieties."

They were still talking about plants five minutes later when a light flashed on the desk, and the woman hurried back and looked at a small hooded screen which came on and magically printed out a message. It was a small readout screen from another keyboard somewhere.

"Mr. Bompensiero says you can go right in now, Miss Martin. Here, let me open the door for you." Joanna saw the woman put a small round metal plate in her hand as she took the door handle. The metal covered the outside of the flat faced door knob. She turned it and the door reacted to the metallic plate and slid sideways into the wall.

Joanna walked into a room that was startlingly different from the others she had seen. On the floor there was no carpet, only a whitish tile. Two straight-backed chairs were placed at the side and front of a desk that looked like World War II surplus oak that hadn't been refinished since. Behind it sat a man in an ancient tilt-back, solid-oak captain's desk chair.

The man in the chair looked up, holding a cigar in his mouth and a scowl on his face.

"Mr. Bompensiero, this is Melody Martin. She called yesterday and we set up an appointment for to-day at this time."

"Yes, Mrs. Lester, thank you." He nodded, dismiss-ing her, and she went back through the door. The man pressed a button on his desk, closing the panel. There was no door knob or opener of any kind on the inside.

"Sit down, Miss Martin," Bompensiero said. His eyes were flint. His dark hair had been cut in a fash-ion of the twenties, almost white-sided, short all over and parted. He looked about thirty years old, but deep frown lines marked his forehead and the corners of his mouth. His loose Hawaiian shirt was covered with pictures of large green parrots. He looked at a paper on his desk.

"Melody Martin, and you heard we had a position open in our research department. How did you find that out?" His stare was frank now, at the point of being unkind.

"One of the girls' rommates told me. A friend of a friend, so I don't even know her name. Mr. Bompensi-ero, I don't want to get anyone in trouble. But if there is a job, I can sure use one."

"Miss Martin, there is no job in research. That is staffed in an entirely different manner. We might

57

have an opening in our advertising department, which would involve PR and modeling. We're looking for a girl who can give us the right image, will become our spokesman and generally do our PR and advertising work for us. Have you ever done any modeling?"

Joanna mentally pulled back and regrouped. He was moving too fast, from mild disinterest to near anger, and now she saw the flush of lechery on his face.

"Yes, as a matter of fact I did model in New York for three years in high fashion, photos, catalog, and live shows. But I got tired of the hectic pace."

"Good, how old are you, Ms. Martin?"

"I'm twenty-eight."

"And about 36-25-37?"

"Close enough and I weigh 115 pounds."

"Well, thank you. I wasn't going to ask you that," he said, with a touch of a smile shifting across his face. "Are you single? I don't see any rings."

"Yes, single."

"Good, take off your clothes, Miss Martin."

"What? I beg your pardon?"

"Take off your clothes. We'll want you in Florida bikinis and maybe topless for some shots, so I need to look at you with your clothes off."

"I'm afraid I can't do that."

"Why? You were a model, weren't you? Certainly you've posed nude before. That shouldn't bother you. Are you hiding some scars or disfigurements?"

"Certainly not. I can show you bikini photos, do some poses, some turns."

"But you won't strip?"

"No, I see no need for that."

"Well, I'm sorry, then there is no job opening. I never buy a horse with a blanket on it, a car without driving it, or a girl with her clothes on. I'll call Mrs. Lester."

"No, wait." Joanna sighed. She looked at him and hated his face already. "Well, if it's an absolute rule. . . ." She took off the white jacket and laid it on the chair, then stood and pulled the light blue cowl-collared cotton top off over her head. She wore no bra, and stood there, nude to the waist, relying on her modeling experience to maintain her composure.

"I imagine this will be far enough. Most men are interested in breasts."

Bompensiero grinned as he stared at her naked torso. He was enjoying it too much. She started to turn when she realized someone had come up behind her. Before she could move, strong hands grabbed her arms and pulled them behind her. She turned and saw only a suit coat button at eye height. The man was huge.

"Now, that we're down to the bare facts of the situation, more or less, let's play a question and answer game," Bompensiero said.

Joanna felt the pressure of the hands on her wrists, then one huge hand caught both her wrists in one crushing grip, and the other hand came in front of her and closed around her left breast.

"Your nerves are very good, ah—Miss Martin, I believe you said. I'm not very good on names. Tell me, exactly what is your assignment here from the Justice Department, and why don't you use your real name, Joanna Tabler?"

She couldn't help but give a short gasp and look at him. Damnit! She had confirmed his guess, or whatever it was. Somehow he knew. She looked down at the big hand gripping her breast and wished he would release her. She wanted to scream at him and scream again, but she knew that would be playing their game.

"Joanna, you haven't answered me. I asked you what your mission was here this time. Oh, yes, we know all about you. A J-6 agent in Justice, so we're moving up in class. The last two of your men who came here were only J-3 and J-4, and both inexperienced and not really very clever. Are you actually trying to infiltrate our organization? Shame, shame. That's not playing the game fair. I'm going to have to call up your Mr. Dan Griggs and reprimand him for this and report him to the referee."

Joanna was past being shocked. Something had gone wrong, very wrong. She knew that there had been two agents assigned to this case, and she hadn't seen either of them lately. Neither had she been given their names for contacts here. Had they been liquidated? Probably. She had certainly stumbled into the big man's trap. But how did they know who she was from a phone call? Then she knew. The pretty etching on the mirror picture in the outer office was in reality a one-way mirror. That's what the wait was about while they ran an I.D. on her. The coffee cup would have speeded up the process with her fingerprints.

The hand over her breast rubbed gently, and she was subtly aware that it was affecting her. She steeled herself against the unwanted caress.

"Mr. Bompensiero, I don't know what you're talking about. I'm so shocked and infuriated by this big gorilla holding me that I'm surprised I can even talk. You tell him to let go of me or I'll scream so loud half of West Palm Beach will be in here."

"No way, pretty tits. We've got soundproofing and automatic doors." He rose from the oak chair and went to where she had been sitting. He opened her purse and dumped everything in it on his desk. Her .38 came rolling out, but thank God she had her cover I.D, not her Justice Department cards.

He examined the I.D. carefully. "Very good. Excellent. An identity card in the name of Melody Martin, with thumb print, picture and state seal. The photostat of your birth certificate on the back is a neat twist. But we know the government can afford the best printing."

He turned toward her and slapped Joanna's right breast, drawing a surprised gasp from her.

"Right now, Joanna, I want you to tell me your exact assignment. What were you supposed to do?"

She looked out the window, and could see the surf breaking on the shore. Joanna wished she were in the water without a care in the world. Like when she and Mark had been in Acapulco. She would think about that, and not about what was happening to her.

Bompensiero slapped her breast again, then bent and kissed it and a moment later he was biting it gently in a way that was more designed to seduce than torture. She realized the man who had been holding her left breast had removed his hand, and now the flint-eyed man was playing with both her breasts. He snapped her nipples until both came erect, expectant, and the excruciating pain produced tears in Joanna's eyes.

"Well, there is a little life in Joanna yet, isn't there? Did I tell you that we know all about you? We broke your cover the first time you were here nearly three years ago. Photographed you, fingerprinted you, had a detailed description. However we did miss the small mole on your left breast." He kissed both her breasts, then slapped them, hard this time, bringing a gasp of pain from Joanna.

The soft warm sand, the beautiful Acapulco beach and that luxurious water, and then the delicious nights with Mark beside her! She had to remember the good times, the good times!

"We have complete dates of your stays at the hotels here in town, which nights, which room numbers, and a list of the phone calls you made, and in one case a detailed copy of your report to Mr. Griggs. We're extremely efficient, Miss Tabler, I assure you."

He bent and kissed her lips before she could turn away.

"Well, well, she is a little touchy today. Kono, see that she goes into the rehab room and check on her tolerances, to all levels of heat and cold. The usual testing that you're so good at. I'm sure she'll be a good addition to our internal executive pool, if they can't use her over in experimental. The usual medical, then if it all checks out, we'll have her on the afternoon boat to the island."

"Yes, sir," Kono said. He caught her wrist and started pulling her toward the door.

"Kono, let the lady put on her clothes first. We don't want to share her goodies with everyone on the whole floor, now, do we?"

Joanna put on her top slowly, then the jacket. She made a dash for the only door she saw with a handle on it, but the handle would not turn. Kono grunted his approval and Bompensiero chuckled.

"We do like them with some spirit, Kono, don't we?"

Joanna Tabler fought the big Hawaiian as he led her out of the room, until he bent down and picked her up and carried her into the hall.

Suddenly everything crashed in around her. The department had been tragically underestimating Preacher Mann for two years. She could see that now. He was highly organized, and vicious. Even his underlings like Bompensiero were shrewed, clever, ruthless and resourceful.

Joanna wouldn't give them the pleasure of seeing her cry, but deep down she wondered if this were that one mistake an agent can make that is absolutely irreversible. It could be. For just a moment she wished she knew where Mark Hardin was. Where had he been heading when the professor called him back to the Stronghold? As soon as she checked in with Dan, he had set up this meeting in West Palm Beach.

Kono pushed open the door and carried her inside a small room that had only a bed, one chair, and a small bath. He kicked the door shut, then dropped her on the bed, tore off his shirt, and kicked out of his pants. Kono didn't believe in underwear. He took off her jacket and pushed the cotton top up around her chin. She clawed at his face but missed and he slapped her so hard her ears were ringing. A moment later she felt him stripping her white pants off.

"Now, little spy, you get your first test, a real *kanaka* treat straight from the Kona coast."

Joanna closed her eyes and set her teeth firmly together. She was determined not to respond in any way.

## Chapter 7

# CHECKING OUT A FORTRESS

Mark slept well for the less than three hours he allowed himself, then woke on Kristi's couch precisely at 6:00 A.M. He took out his "basic Florida" outfit, a wild print shirt, white pants and white shoes. As he dressed Mark debated with himself whether he should take his two suitcases with him. That way it would be a clean break and there could be no danger to Kristi. In the end the leave-them-here vote won and he slipped out of the house at 6:15 heading for an eatery and then to find a car rental agency where he could get wheels for a week without any elaborate identification.

Breakfast was eggs, grits, bacon, and three big pancakes. David Red Eagle would scream, but he could clean up Mark's eating habits later. The Penetrator caught a cab and cruised past Florida Home Federal building where he saw his car on the street where he had left it—only now it had a traffic citation on it. Mark knew the rig was being watched, from any of a hundred windows that faced on it from both sides of the street. The big Florida Home Federal building had to be the hoodlum's nest, but where in the structure? He'd have to do a lot more looking around before he could come up with an attack plan. Mark had decided intuitively that this type of an operation had to be the biggest game in town—which meant Preacher Mann. No one else could function the way these boys did, and be in competition with the Preacher. So this had to be the base of the crime boss. At least one of the home bases.

The Penetrator found a side-street, rundown rental firm called West Palm Budget Rentals, and talked them out of a three-year-old Mustang for twelve dollars a day. They didn't ask for any I.D. and Mark didn't volunteer any. He drove the car for ten miles around town and along the beach to get used to it and see how it handled. It didn't have as much pickup as a Pinto, but it would have to do. At least he wouldn't have to worry about making any high-speed chases with the rustic Mustang.

Mark arrived at the main entrance to the Florida Home building at five minutes to eight with a gaggle of secretaries, junior executives, salesmen, and flunkies going up in the elevator to the various floors. Eight was the top. The elevator did not have any buttons for floors nine, ten or eleven. He'd seen lots of patchwork buildings in New York made that way, so he went down and tried another elevator, but it had the same buttons as the first. Mark checked in the lobby and at last found the last elevator on the end which said "floors 1 through 9." He prowled the corridors and sitting rooms of half of the floors as he worked up toward the ninth. He had used the stairs for most of his trip, and had found nothing but routine offices, hundreds of medical-dental suites, small businesses, a literary agency, two small regional magazines and dozens of small sales organizations.

Mark went back to the ground level, walked through the savings and loan offices, then the other streetside businesses. They all seemed perfectly normal.

On the tenth floor Carlos Blanco sat behind a TV monitoring system. There were nine screens in front of him, but he watched only number seven. The man was big enough, Carlos thought, but with the dark glasses and the sailing cap on, it was difficult to tell who he was. Every man in the organization had been alerted to watch out for the Penetrator. They had it verbally and in writing. There also was a stipulation that the persons who were responsible for capturing or killing the wanted man, would receive or share in a fifty-thousand-dollar bonus!

Carlos had been alert over his monitors ever since he heard the news. And the report indicated the Penetrator had been outside the building in the early-morning hours. Carlos had spotted the tall dark man on his second screen early. During one hour he had seen the same man on the corridor and lobby cameras at least a dozen times. The man seemed to be making a complete tour of each floor. He was not a city inspector. They always had plenty of notice when such official visits were made for the required look-overs.

Carlos glanced down at the sketch of the Penetrator that had been furnished to him by a guy who had seen the man close up several times. It was too bad the eye-witness had not been a better artist, Carlos thought.

Now the man was talking to the main lobby guard. Carlos watched the conversation and dialed the guard's station. When the guard finished talking he picked up the phone.

"Who was that?" Carlos asked in Cuban-accented Spanish.

"He didn't say. Just asked me how to get to the tenth and eleventh floors. I told him they were leased by a separate research company with private entrances. The usual line."

"Did he believe you?"

"I doubt it. He has the look of a wolf about him."

As Carlos watched the man on his lobby screen, two uniformed guards came into the lobby on some job and moved toward the big man in the white pants. For a moment Carlos thought he detected indecision from the way the man's shoulders moved and his head turned. Then the big man walked up and began talking to a gentleman in his sixties who was dressed extremely well. That confused Carlos. Had the man only been looking for a friend, someone he had been waiting for? Carlos settled back, swiftly checked the other screens for problems, security or otherwise, then came back to the pair near the main fountain. Both were talking now, and it seemed plain that they did know each other.

Carlos called quickly for Henry.

"Get in here and take over the board," he snapped. "And see that pair on number eight? I want you to track them, tell me whatever they do and where they go. I'll keep in touch with you on radio, tac five."

Carlos straightened his tie and ran for the elevators.

Below in the lobby, Mark had seen the pair of security guards coming and felt sure they were heading for him. Later he realized he had overreacted, perhaps due to too little sleep. At any rate he had looked for a friendly, or at least not an angry, countenance and, when he spotted a man near the fountain, he moved.

Mark walked quickly to him and grabbed his hand.

"Charlie! Jesus, it's been years since I've seen you, but I'd remember your face anywhere, even if it is a little older than when we were in the service together."

The man had not winced at the firm handclasp, nor did he show surprise.

"I think you may be mistaken," the man said. He was six feet tall, 165 pounds, sixty-one or two, and his hair covered his ears in the current style, with long sideburns. He had heavy gray eyebrows, a strong nose and thin lips in a well sun-tanned face.

Mark shook his head. "Hell no, Charlie. I'd know you in a blacked-out coal mine at midnight." Mark looked at the two security guards. They had stopped and were pointedly not looking his way. One of them used a small handi-talkie radio.

"Young man, my name is Herbert John Hofmann, and I live in Del Mar, California. I'm here looking for some small businesses I might buy. I'm sorry, but I've never seen you before in my life."

"Now, Charlie, so I owe you fifty bucks. That's no reason to be mad. Damnit, Charlie, I'll pay you back right now, if that's what makes you mad. How about a drink first, then we can talk. There must be a bar around here somewhere." Mark had carefully analyzed the man: solid, a business type, athletic, a bit reserved. The Penetrator knew he couldn't push too far.

"I really don't understand. I have a very good eye

69

for faces, I've only been in town for two days combining a bit of a vacation while I look over some investments. . . ."

"Now I've got it," Mark said, guessing. "La Jolla. I've seen you in La Jolla, right?"

Herbert Hofmann lifted his gray brows in surprise. "Well, that is possible. I lived there for twelve years." His brown eyes sparkled for just a minute. "Is this a joke, a put on? Did somebody tell you to do this? Some friend of mine?"

Mark shook his head. "Come on, Charlie. Remember that party in La Jolla at the fantastic Earl Gagosian mansion up on La Jolla Farms Road? You were there with a cute little redhead." Hofmann chuckled, and Mark saw that the threat of his bolting was past. He glanced at the guards who walked in his direction again but they were not watching him. A smart tactic.

"Now, how about that drink and we'll get the old times all straightened out?" Mark asked.

"I'm sorry, I just don't have the time. But I assure you, my name is Herbert Hofmann, with two n's. I'm from Del Mar and I've never seen you before."

"You're single now, right, with two or three kids all grown up."

"Well, nearly right. One son is an attorney, and the other in sales. My daughter is in graduate school. Now, if this is an interview, it's certainly an unusual kind."

Mark watched the guards pass them and head for a man who seemed to be wearing nothing but a long raincoat. No pants legs showed under the coat.

"Now, Mr. Hofmann, you really don't remember me? Mel Hornbrook from San Diego? I'm sure I saw you at that party, but I'd had a few, you know. Maybe I did get the name mixed up."

Hofmann laughed. His brown eyes crinkled at the corners. "At first I thought you were a shill or a pickpocket but there didn't seem to be anybody working with you, so I eliminated that. Really, I'm not Charlie, and I don't remember seeing you in La Jolla, not even at the Tennis Club. Do you play?"

"No, I'm afraid not. Well, Mr. Hofmann, I'm sorry. If I've held you up from something important, forgive me."

Hofmann stared at him a moment, his face grim, then he nodded and smiled. "Hornbrook, and I'm sure that isn't your name. I've been conned by some of the best, and you're good. You evidently needed someone here to talk to, to confuse someone or cover up something, and I must have looked like a good prospect. I hope it worked for you. Now I really must go." Herbert Hofmann took one more look at Mark, smiled, then turned and walked away, his back straight, his light blue expensive suit perfectly tailored. He didn't look back.

Mark saw the security guards swoop down on the man in the raincoat just as he put his hands in the pockets and whipped the coat wide open. He wore nothing under the coat. They grabbed him and hurried him away.

Mark walked around the fountain, found no one particularly interested in him, and headed for the side door that opened into Ashford street.

Carlos Blanco had watched Mark in his talk with the gray-haired man and wasn't sure if it had been planned or not. At first the other man had looked a bit surprised, then Carlos edged closer enough to hear

71

the talking about La Jolla, and he reasoned that it was not uncommon for people to see someone they knew when they came to Florida. But the young man was still a suspect. Carlos lifted the small two-way radio and alerted Matt and Joey on the Ashforth street entrance.

"Yes, Matt, that's the one, just leaving, about six feet two. White pants, captain's hat. Follow, detain, question and if necessary use maximum force which is authorized."

"Gotcha," Matt said and fell into step behind the big man. He signaled Joey on the other side of the street and they moved along slowly behind the Florida print shirt and white pants. This was just his kind of meat—a little action for a change.

Twenty feet after he left the big building, Mark sensed that he was being tailed. He examined a store window and spotted the man behind him, about Mark's size, with big ears, crew cut hair and a white knit shirt, a Mexican or Cuban. Mark was delighted with the attention. With one-on-one or three-on-one, he might get some information. He walked down the street to the alley, darted into it and sprinted for a big trash bin fifty feet down the narrow strip of cement. Mark slid out of sight behind the dumpster just before Matt ran to the end of the alley and looked into the morning shadows.

Matt grinned. The big gringo was frightned; he had run and now hid, hoping no one would follow him. Surprise, surprise, big gringo. You gonna get your ass stomped good! Matt walked down the center of the alley, watching both sides, knowing the white pants and white shoes had to be near this end of the block-long alley. But where?

He heard Joey enter the alley behind him, his hard leather boots making ominous sounds on the cement.

Matt wanted this one. He waved Joey back, to stay in reserve if he were needed. Matt moved another six steps and saw the stranger crouching near the front edge of the dumpster.

"You set up this meet, buster. What do you want?" Mark asked, his voice neutral. He stood now facing the other man a dozen feet away.

Matt missed the implied undertone of neutrality, mistaking it for fear.

"Who are *you*, and what are you doing here?" the Cuban asked.

"I'm a citizen, and I want to go on walking down this alley. Any objections?"

"Plenty. Do you have any identification?"

"Plenty, do you?" Mark saw the second man come within ten yards of them and stop on a signal from the first.

"Only two-to-one? What's the matter, no skill or no guts?"

"White trash, I take you with one hand, any day!" Matt spit it out, his excitement rising.

Mark didn't have time to waste on these punks, but they might give him some information. He reached in his pocket and took out a small ball without the men seeing him. It was about the size of a Bing cherry. Suddenly he threw it against the cement wall where the backup man lounged. The small gas bomb exploded against the wall, showering the man with fragments of the plastic cover and dumping a full load of the gas into his face and lungs. It wasn't lethal but the man would be unconscious for a half hour.

Matt looked in surprise and dug for the .38 under his sport shirt.

"Better not try it," Mark barked at him, his .45 automatic already zeroed in on Matt's chest.

Matt's hand stopped still under his shirt.

"Take out your toy and lay it on the cement," Mark ordered. He watched as Matt did it. Matt shook his head, not quite sure how the tables had turned on him so quickly, so completely. He had been confident, in control, with a backup man. Now he was alone, weaponless and with a .45 trained on him. The guy must be Mafia. The damn Italians were trying to take over the territory again.

Mark came toward Matt and smiled. "You think you're pretty good, amigo? You're nothing but a dumb, bungling amateur. I made you ten feet after you hit the bricks behind me. You're too stupid to live." Mark walked toward him, the .45 aimed at the man's head. Matt's brown eyes came up and never left Mark's eyes.

"Who do you work for, dead man. What outfit?"

Matt looked away, then he lunged at Mark, who sidestepped and brought the gun down across Matt's head as he surged past. The guard writhed on the pavement, got up, holding his bleeding head, then charged Mark. The hoodlum had guessed right. Mark wasn't going to shoot unless he had to. He was looking for information, not a body count.

Matt came head down, fists flailing like a windmill. Mark jumped aside, kicked the man in the stomach, straightening him up, then slammed the side of his hand hard into the side of Matt's neck, driving him to the cement again.

This time Matt didn't get up. He vomited, then

stared at Mark in wonder and hatred. "Who the hell are you?" Matt asked.

Mark tossed him an arrowhead. "Give this to the boss and tell him I'm still here. He missed me at the airport and last night he missed again outside the store, but when I come for him, I won't miss, I never do. You tell the Preacher Mann to get ready to die!"

## Chapter 8

## FINDING A BIRD

The Penetrator faded from the alley into the next street, went over two more blocks and found a small cafe where he sat in back, watched the door and nursed a cup of black coffee. No one had followed him. He had pricked their skins and they retaliated, with sudden and deadly force. So he had the right building and the right location, the top floors. Only how do you assault a downtown skyscraper?

Given time he could research the place and go through some of the connecting doors or stairwells into the upper floors, but he was sure Preacher Mann had all those access routes carefully watched and heavily protected. There could be no surprise element. He needed an assault that would be quick, give him a ninety percent chance of walking away, yet would be highly effective.

So it had to be a vertical assault, a favorite military technique, and in this case the only reasonable one. There was too much ground cover, there were too many civilian "sheep" and built in defenses for a frontal attack. He'd go through the roof, not original, but certainly effective, and he'd have a good line of egress. All he needed was the right firepower and a bird. Finding the fly-boy who might do the job was another problem.

The second edition of the morning papers had splashed across the front pages the story of the Penetrator. Some reporter had done his homework. The story tied the flint arrowheads in with the Penetrator, then dug into the files for background and history on the Penetrator as a crime fighter. It was a sympathetic treatment of Mark's campaign, probably the most positive that Mark had seen in all his years of action. The one big question the story opened was, who was the Penetrator hunting in West Palm Beach?

A front-page picture of the burning car with inserts of the arrowheads and burned-up weapons, covered six columns. The last paragraph of the story quoted the local chief of police as saying that the Penetrator was not a Robin Hood or a folk hero to him.

"The man is a criminal with more than a hundred felony warrants out for his arrest. To me he's only another wanted man who is armed and considered highly dangerous. He will be treated as such. Now that he's blundered into my jurisdiction, he will be promptly brought to justice."

Mark put down the paper and thought about Kristi. There was no telling how this might affect her if she made the connection. On an impulse he drove to her apartment, watched it a few minutes, saw no lurking figures, and went inside. There was no reception waiting for him. He thought Preacher Mann might have found some magical way to trace him to her, some connection. Mark quickly gathered up his belongings, left and locked the door behind behin. Now, he hoped that the pretty school teacher would be out of danger.

Mark locked his suitcase and his clothes in the trunk of the Mustang and drove to the airport. He left the passenger terminal area and wheeled to the commercial flying end of the field. Mark found two helicopter services. Both were large, with several choppers on the pads in front. He drifted into one of the hangars and talked to a workman at a repair bench. Mark said he was looking for a small firm, maybe some struggling jock with just one bird and a fist full of debts.

The mechanic grinned and said his buddy had just such an outfit. He was almost aways broke. "I help him out sometimes nights and Sundays to keep his bird flying," the mechanic said. "He's an all right, standup guy. Flew choppers in Vietnam. It's the Ralston Flying Service down in building 24 A, way down at the end. Down there in the low-rent district. If nobody's there just leave a message or wait. Bud's the whole outfit, does everything himself."

Marked thanked the mechanic and drove toward the far end of the airport.

A sign on building 24A read: RALSTON FLYING SERVICE. A helicopter sat on a pad in front of the building, and did not appear to have a hangar. It was an older, four-place rig that had seen a lot of hard service. Mark looked over the chopper, then walked to a small door in the side of the building and found himself in an office no bigger than a motel living room. The guy behind the small counter was in his late twenties, maybe thirty, with a blond crew cut, light blue eyes that seemed to be laughing and even, white teeth.

"Like my bird? Want to buy her? She don't look none too swift, but she's sound and in top shape."

Mark shook his head.

"Well, hell. You can't win them all. Bud Ralston's the name."

"I'm looking for a short charter ride."

"I'll fly you anywhere, anytime—as long as it's for cash."

"How long did you fly in 'Nam?"

"Three years. Got my belly full of being shot at and enough shrapnel in my ass to come home."

Mark held out his hand. "I owe you some thanks. I've always had a lot of respect for you eggbeater jockeys. More than once you boys came charging in and got me out of waist deep trouble. I spent some time in 'Nam myself."

They looked frankly at one another, then both laughed.

"Harry phoned, said you were asking about me. Thought you were looking for a cheap ride. But I don't think you are. Are you hot or is the ride illegal?"

"A little of both. All I want you to do is drop me off on top of a downtown office building, and then come back and pick me up on a signal."

"Without a permit?"

"I'm not very popular with your police force."

"An illegal landing is a big bucks fine."

Bud Ralston watched this tall, dark man a moment. He liked what he saw. Honest, straight, would have made a hell of a good cop. But there was a twinge of doubt. It was illegal, but how far did that go?

"Is anybody going to get hurt on this mission? I mean, I don't mind a landing rap, but I don't want to get mixed up in anything involving a felony."

"Yes, Mr. Ralston, someone might get hurt, but if they do it will be because they have been hurting a lot of other people for a long time with impunity."

"That's what I was afraid of."

"Ralston, have you ever heard of Preacher Mann?"

"Hell, yes. He's big daddy. A black who knows he's boss. He can do just about anything he wants. . . ." Ralston looked up. "You going in against him, alone?"

"Just a social call."

"Through the roof. Fat chance. It would take an M-16 and a couple of dozen fraggers! Damn! So there might be some shooting."

"There might be, if they shoot first."

Ralston leaned on the counter, kicked at the supports and grinned at Mark. "You make it sound almost like another war, the good guys against the bad. Man, you going in there alone?"

"In a way. But in 'Nam we used to say a fragger used right was the best buddy a grunt ever had." Mark watched him. "One condition on my offer, Ralston. You don't tell anybody we even talked, or that I mentioned the Preacher. Agreed?"

"Hell, yes. He'd snuff us both quick. No sweat there."

"What's your taxi driver fee?"

"My rate is five hundred."

Mark shook his head. "No way, this is a combat mission. I'll give you three thousand, take it or leave it."

"Three thous. . . ." Bud looked up at Mark. "You're not with the F.B.I. or other Feds or anything?"

"No."

"But you're not Mafia or the other outside hoods either?"

"Right, I'm freelance, like you. Deal?"

"Damn right! I need the cash. You got yourself a taxi driver. When do we lift off?"

"Later tonight. I'll be here at midnight." Mark took from his pocket a roll he had transferred from his money belt earlier. He counted out thirty new one-hundred-dollar bills.

But Ralston shook his head as he picked up the cash. "Mister, I haven't seen that much real money in five years!"

"Put it away. Don't flash it around. When we get back here you may have visitors from the local law. All you have to do is swear that I forced you to take me on the ride. Say I had your family kidnapped or threatened to do that. Make up a good story. Then you won't get into my trouble."

Mark shook hands and left quickly before Ralston could change his mind. He went to a small restaurant on the highway and had a quick meal, then replenished his cash supply from his clothes suitcase and checked over his arms bag. From where he had parked under a palm tree he could see the beach. Wave after cool wave drove in from the Atlantic, splashing onto the warm sand. It was a beach, but it didn't have the sparkle and excitement of a good Southern California breaker coming in at Malibu or Laguna Beach. For just a moment he wished he were body surfing at Crescent Bay in Laguna.

Mark shook out of the dream and plotted out the weapons he would need for the assault. He decided to use the Mossburg shotgun, which now lay disassembled in the suitcase, white phosphorous smoke grenades for fire and cover and some old-fashioned fraggers. He'd also have his hand guns, the High Standard .22, his small, trusty .45 Star automatic, and Ava.

He thought it through again and was reasonably sure that there would be no innocent "sheep" of any kind on the top two floors of the crime lord's headquarters. Since he had no idea about the layout of the target, he couldn't plan out his attack. He'd simply be on a search and destroy mission, going for a shock effect, destroying and knocking down as much of the nerve center as he could.

That decided, Mark headed for a shaded telephone booth so he could call the professor and check in. He dialed a remembered number in Los Angeles. An operator answered and he gave the proper code word, which allowed the answering service girl to punch a forwarding button on her board which automatically dialed a pre-set and secret number. A phone rang in the Stronghold. It was picked up on the second ring.

"Yes?" It was Professor Haskins' voice.

"Good afternoon, Professor, and greetings from the sunshine."

They tried not to use real names in telephone conversations, in case of taps on either end.

"We here had hoped that you might call. It seems that our government man in Washington is most unhappy with us. He found out about your operation there from his news wire. Says he has a special project of his own going down in that area, and he doesn't want you tampering with it."

"His timing is lousy. Did he say what it was?"

"No, but I'd guess it's the same as yours."

"Do we have any more data on the big man?"

"Not much. My contacts around the country simply have no more information. The Washington man did say that his top girl was sent there two days ago, and that she has not made her mandatory phone contacts. He has no idea what her problem is, but it is not typical of her. He wanted you to know that she is in your area. Will that present you with any problems?"

"Not unless our revivalist friend talks to her. What was she supposed to do here?"

"He indicated it would be an infiltration."

"Sounds like trouble if she's working on Mann. He is brilliant, with an outstanding organization here. If she tried to infiltrate there and hasn't been heard from, she probably didn't make it."

"Which is bad news."

"With this man, it's extremely bad, Professor. Tell your Washington friend I'll do all I can for the cause and try to find his girl. I'm paying a visit to our friend tonight, and we'll see what happens from there. Keep digging on any more background."

"The only new item we have is a rumor we keep hearing about—a deluxe, exclusive jet-set type of call-girl operation. This man provided the girls in any shape, size, or age and with almost any talent, from an opera singer to a high school cheer leader to a scuba diver or tennis player. They are delivered by private jet anywhere in the world and the price is fantastic."

"Sounds like a logical expansion for this bird," Mark said. They talked a bit more, then said goodbye.

Mark was thinking ahead. There was little more he could do until later that night. He drove to a shaded street by a small park and closed and locked the car doors. Then he sprawled on the green grass in the shade and had a three hour nap. When he woke it was just after 5:00. Mark drove to a sidewalk telephone booth and called Kristi. He had memorized the number before he left. He wanted to check to be sure she was not bothered, and to apologize for not coming for dinner.

The phone rang three times, then someone picked it up.

"Hello?"

"Kristi?"

"Yes, this is Kristi, who is this?"

"Doug,"

He heard her gasp. "Don't come! Some men are here who. . . ." Her voice soared into a scream. The phone was silent for a moment, then a man's voice came through.

"If this is Doug, you must listen carefully. Your little friend Kristi is in serious trouble. She helped you last night to escape from us. And now she is in considerable pain. Do you understand what I mean, Doug?"

A flood of anger, frustration, and fury cascaded over Mark and he realized again he had caused someone suffering for only being near him, for being in the wrong place when he was there. He worked a few seconds to control his emotions and his voice. Then his voice came, cold, sinister.

"I don't know what you're talking about, whoever you are. But if that girl is harmed in any way, *any way*, I'll find out exactly who did it, and strip his skin from his flesh an inch at a time. The pain will be so tremendous, he'll scream for the release of a quick death. Do you read me?"

"Don't be ridiculous. We're only reasoning with the girl. She says she's never seen you before last night, that you forced her to help you. Isn't that ridiculous?"

A scream sounded over the phone. "Now I'm afraid that even she is starting to get emotional about this."

"I have an expert memory for voices," Mark said. "If she is harmed at all, even scratched, you're dead!" Mark hung up gently and stood staring at the side of the phone booth. The torture, the violation, the death of innocents who touched his life only to find him an eventual poison to them, nothing could cure. He wanted to smash the phone booth into rubble, to tear the offending telephone out by its root wires, to scream until he was voiceless. But he didn't. He kept staring at the booth wall until the red tide of instant hatred washed over him and left. Kristi? How could they have traced her so quickly? What did they have to go on? He relived the chase scene, guessed there were three men at the car or nearby. Then he figured it out. Her license plate. One of the men had caught the license plate number as the car sped through the stop light. That was all they needed for a quick check of the vehicle registration office and they had name, current address and auto make. Then they had waited for her to come home. He should have thought about the possibility last night, or even this morning. He could have moved her to a hotel for the night or for a week.

If only. . . .

Mark left the phone booth and drove to the beach. He stared at the waves and walked along the sand. He had no illusions about Kristi. She would be dead by now, long before he could even try to help her. Preacher Mann's men were cool, efficient, and worst of all, intelligent. They functioned within parameters, but used their initiative where it was needed.

By now he was sure the Preacher's people had her apartment well covered and an ambush set up, so that he would never even get to her door before he would be riddled with a dozen bullets.

Kristi had served her purpose for them; she had baited the trap. They only needed her to answer the phone and to scream. After that she became not only a liability, but an embarrassment. She had warned him, and he was sure that in doing so she had died less quickly, and with much more pain and torture than she might have otherwise. She must have died without even knowing his name, or understanding what he was doing.

Mark kicked the sand in frustration. Kristi was a soldier, an unwilling, unknowing pawn in the fight against crime. And she had been killed in the line of duty for the good of the whole army. She had helped him escape and in doing so had sealed her own death. But she would be avenged, not out of hatred, but through an effective action against an entrenched enemy. And it would start tonight!

Mark got back in his Mustang and drove into the business section of West Palm Beach. Suddenly he wanted to be around people, to watch them laugh and have fun, and enjoy life. Last night Kristi had been one of them. Now she was gone. Mark Hardin put his head on the steering wheel and wished that he could cry.

## Chapter 9

# DEATH FROM THE SKY

The Penetrator arrived at the airport at 11:30 P.M. He now wore a set of all black Resistweve clothes: a tight-fitting tee shirt with long sleeves of the medium-weight material, and black pants. The tighter the fit the more resistant the cloth was, the maker had told him. He locked the Mustang and looked around the far end of the airport. He saw nothing out of place, no idling engines, no parked cars that looked suspicious. After a wait he went silently to the small window in the Ralston Flying Service office and looked in. The pilot was there alone.

Mark went in without knocking.

Ralston sat behind the small desk, his feet resting on the corner, his hands laced behind his head. He grinned when he saw Mark.

"Evening. I'm just trying to figure out which of my bills to pay, and when I do, how I explain where I got the cash." He stood and moved to shake hands. "Ready to go?"

"No, too early. You have any visitors today?"

Ralson looked up, surprised. "Yeah, matter of fact I did. All the chopper pads in town had a visitor, a sickly-looking, sandy-haired kid who works over at the transient hangar."

"I know the one. We've met."

"Said he was taking a survey of services in case some customer asked about getting a chopper. But he also slipped in a casual question about any charters by a big dark guy like you. Oh, he threw it away—said one of the other chopper places lost the job and asked him to ask me if I got it and how much the cheapskate actually paid."

"What did you say?"

"I asked him to send me some business. Said I hadn't seen the tall dark guy, but I'd take him if I found him. I cried a little about how bad business was and offered him ten bucks to bird dog customers to me. He was polite at least until I told him I hadn't had a charter for three days and didn't expect one."

"Thanks. It could mean they were thinking of having a reception committee on top."

"I've been in that kind of a spot before."

"True, and you know this bird of yours is a sitting mud duck if they have any rifles up there."

"Right, man, but who wants to live forever? It's been so long since anybody has shot at me, that I kind of miss it."

Mark stared at Ralston for sixty seconds, then accepted it. For a moment he thought it might be an elaborate double cross, but Ralston's eyes never wavered. "Maybe they're just trying to cover all the bases. If they're convinced I haven't rented a bird, we're home free." Mark said it to reassure Ralston as much as himself. The moment Ralston lifted the chopper off the pad somebody would hear it and could report to Preacher Mann. A phone call would get to the eleventh floor long before Mark could. He brushed it all aside. If there were watchers on the roof, they would probably fall into familiar time slots, six to twelve, and twelve to six. He'd hit them at 1:30.

The two men played gin rummy for an hour, and Mark lost a dollar and a half at a penny a point. Then they went out to the helicopter.

Ralston did a double-take at the army shoulder bag the Penetrator carried from his Mustang, and he showed more interest when Mark took out the Mossberg ATP 8S riot shotgun. He kept the long gun beside his leg until he slid it into the chopper. They had moved so far without lights, and a minimum of noise. Ralston said he could take off blind. He was farthest from the tower and they probably wouldn't notice him. He stared in wonder at the shoulder bag and its hidden contents.

"I didn't know this was going to be World War Three!" Ralston said.

"It won't. I don't have any atomic bombs. I just take what I think I might need. If I don't use it all, I don't mind dragging it back with me."

Ralston took a deep breath. "You damned grunts always did have all the fun. We just came in and tried to pick up the leftovers."

They took off with no problem, skirted the end of the airport and, without lights, headed for the downtown section.

"So far they've got me on three violations: no running lights, unauthorized takeoff, and a no-permit downtown landing."

"Any police choppers in this area?" Mark asked.

Ralston shook his head in the dim light from the instruments. "Nope, we can't afford any."

"Good. I'll put this strobe light on top of the savings and loan building pointing upward. You can home in on it fast. Make a sweep over the place every ten minutes. When I want to get out of there, I'll have a red flare burning near the strobe. Got it?"

"Yeah." There was a break in his voice. "This sure as hell feels like old times! You know, for the pure gut thrills of it, there just isn't anything like a good shooting war, even a little one. I kind of miss the days in 'Nam."

"General George Patton agreed with you. He said something like: 'Next to war, all of man's other activities pale into insignificance.' War is exciting, and brutal, a thrill a minute—just as long as you keep on living."

"Yeah, there's always that. Look alive now, target coming up in about two minutes."

Mark checked his arms. His silent, deadly Ava in the belt holster had red-tipped killer darts. His .22 High Standard was on the other side in a clip on rig. The leather shoulder holster carried his small-sized Star .45. He had death darts only in Ava for quiet work. That was if he got onto the roof and could make a silent entry.

The Mossberg riot shotgun had eight rounds in the magazine, alternately loaded with double-ought .33 caliber pellets, and #4 buck. It was an ideal room-to-room combat situation sweeper. You could get sloppy and lucky and still blow away everything in sight with one round. Inside the bag he had twenty extra 3-inch Magnum 00B rounds for the Mossberg, as well as his old-fashioned M-3 fragmentation grenades and six white phosphorous smoke grenades.

They came in at rooftop level to the tall building, ready for a quick landing, rapid off-loading and fast getaway. Mark opened the outside door now and had one foot on the landing skid, the Mossberg cradled in his arms and the shoulder bag around his back. The chopper veered to miss an antenna, then settled on the roof. Before it touched, Mark dropped the other foot to the black tar, closed the chopper door and waved at Ralston who pulled out the throttle and lifted off at once. So far no greeting party.

Mark placed the battery-operated strobe light on the roof where they had landed, then ran for the nearest ventilator opening. He pushed behind it and checked the rest of the roof. This was when they should hit him, just after his bird left. Man-sized outcroppings loomed in the darkness. Mark ran to one, found it locked. With his pics he opened the hotel door-style lock and was inside within thirty seconds, the silent Ava in his right hand as he went into the dark stairwell. He left the outside door open and felt his way downward.

At the bottom of the straight flight of stairs he touched the door. It had an inside push-type lock. The Penetrator twisted the knob, pushed open the door and looked out a small crack. This was floor eleven.

The hall was dimly lighted. He saw no one, so Mark stepped into the alley, thumbed the safety forward on the Mossberg, and held the dart gun ready as he headed for the first room. The door was unlocked. He slipped inside and turned on the light. He found nothing. It was some kind of a meeting room.

As he eased open the door to leave, the back of a roving guard in mufti sauntered past. Mark lifted Ava and coughed.

The guard whirled, his hand dragging for a .38 at his belt.

"Don't try it or you're dead," Mark said.

"My God! The Penetrator. I'm dead either way." He jerked the pistol from his holster and had it half way up when Mark pulled Ava's trigger. A faint hissing sound was all they heard, then the small dart rammed through the man's shirt. The needlelike dart point penetrated a half inch of flesh and the ram-jet force injected two cc's of deadly curarine poison into his chest. The gun faltered and stopped rising. His fingers didn't have enough strength to pull and the weapon fell to the floor just before the big guard in the finely tailored suit slumped to the hallway, dead within ten seconds.

Mark checked him. He carried no radio equipment, no buzzers or security sending devices.

The next room revealed nothing of value, and Mark moved quickly through a series of half a dozen more which seemed to be offices of some sort, but just what their purpose was he couldn't determine. One room had only a bed, wash stand and dresser, almost like a hotel room. He hadn't consciously been searching for Joanna but, if she tried to infiltrate, this would be the logical place to start—the only place he knew. So he wouldn't be shooting up the place blind—he would make sure of his targets. For just a moment a cold breeze touched him. The international call-girl setup—would they try to force Joanna into such a scheme, or would there be some worse fate for a spy and a government agent? Mark was determined that if he didn't find her here, he would keep going until he did. In the next office he found bookkeeping equipment and, in a locked inner drawer, he discovered three small ledgers. Mark took them, stowing them under the grenades in his shoulder bag. This time when he checked the hallway before going out, he found two men bending over the dead guard. It was too great a range for Ava. Mark tried one silent dart, but saw it fall short. He pulled the Star .45 automatic and steadied in on one of the men and fired, dropping him. Then Mark snapped three quick shots at the other and blew him away.

Now it was open warfare. Mark ran for the stairs he had seen, heading downward. He met one man running up who Mark death-darted without missing a stride. At the door two more men came in, both with handguns out. Mark lifted the Mossberg and blew them both through the door with one round of the double ought .33 caliber cluster of fifteen pellets. Quickly Mark pumped in another round. In the hallway on floor ten he found more activity. He darted into one room across the hall, then flipped a fragmentation grenade down the hall. The crunching varrrumph! explosion spread death and shrapnel all over. Mark jumped into the hall before the smoke settled and found no one standing. It was a search and destroy mission now.

He wanted to find Preacher Man and waste him, but so far the tall black man had been out of sight. Mark threw a white phosphorous grenade into the room he had just left, the office of some minor executive. Phosphorous burns so hotly that nothing can extinguish it. A grenade explodes in a shower of granules and blobs of burning phosphorous that will

95

burn through a couch, a two inch board, or a human body. It sticks to anything and burns with a white-hot brilliant heat and at the same time gives off clouds of thick white smoke.

The Penetrator threw two more of his phosphorous grenades into empty offices, hoping he was destroying something valuable to the enemy. Back in the hall he had just turned to clear it the other way when something hit him in the shoulder and spun him around. It was a glancing shot and it drove him to his knees. The Mossberg came up in a well-schooled reflex action and he fired once, blowing a grinning gunman behind him in half. The man had been leveling in with his .45 to finish off the job. The .45 slug must have slanted off Mark's Resistweve shirt, he concluded, and now his shoulder ached like it had been broken.

He pumped another round into the Mossberg and swept the hallway, then ran to the stairway. Two men were coming down. Ava dropped them silently before they knew what happened and he paused and reloaded the Mossberg magazine, filling it to the limit of seven rounds. The doorway on the top floor was open slightly and he edged it open farther and attracted a round from a handgun slamming past him. He peered around the door and saw a woman fire at him again, the slug missing. She ran into a room.

Mark fired one round from the Mossberg down the hall to discourage door openings, ran behind it to the woman's room and threw a fragger through the open door, heard the explosion, then the woman's plaintive screams in a death agony.

The Penetrator threw two more white phosphorous grenades into fancy offices, tossed in blue flint arrowheads and then looked into the hall. A concentration of small arms fire struck the doorway and wall, forcing him back inside. He peered around the door molding at floor level and saw three doors open into the hall, each with a man hiding behind it and firing. It was a nice defensive gimmick. White smoke poured into the hall. Mark edged the Mossberg around the doorway and triggered off one shot, then pumped in a second round and fired it, listening to the big .33 caliber slugs riddle the doors. He threw a fragger down the hall and, with the explosion, was on his feet, running. He heard screams of pain and surprise. His ears still rang with the sound of the explosions in the confined space. Something moved ahead of him and Mark fired another round of the double ought buck and charged toward the door leading to the roof stairs. He almost made it. One half-dead man in pajama bottoms staggered from behind a doorway and fired his .38 in one swift motion. Mark's .45 slug thundered into the man's torso, shocking him back three feet before he fell, his chest already spouting blood.

Mark knew he was hit again even as he fired. The .38 slug caught him on the right side, but at too much of an angle to penetrate the Resistweve, slanted off and in the process cracked two ribs. Mark groaned at the impact, rolled one more fragger down the hall and staggered up the stairs after locking the door from the steps' side.

On the roof he lit a highway fuse and threw it near the blinking strobe light. He left a flint arrowhead beside them, then settled behind a large air vent, his Mossberg zeroed in on the door leading to the roof. It never opened. Before he knew what had happened, he was taking small arms fire from behind. Mark swung around the vent and realized they had come up the other roof access stairs. Mark took his next to last fragger and threw it at the door. It went off four feet in front of the opening.

He heard the *whup-whup* of the chopper coming in. Mark brought up the Mossberg and sent a shower of hot lead into the doorway and quieted the new fire. He'd put it into the stairway, which should prevent anyone from having a good shot at the chopper.

He used the last round in the Mossberg and then stormed twenty feet closer to the roof stairs to the protection of another air vent. The W.P. sailed straight and true and exploded inside the stairs. Mark saw one man lift up just as the "Willy Peter" went off. The man screamed and staggered onto the roof. His bare chest was pocked with burning splotches of white phosphorous. He dug at them, tried to get the sticky substance off his flesh, only to find his fingers burning too. One spot burned hotly at his neck as Mark watched. The man screamed once more, clutching at his throat, bright red blood gushing through two holes in his neck from ruptured carotid arteries as he stumbled toward the stairs and fell back into the smoke.

The chopper landed on the roof.

The Penetrator rushed to it, dumped the bag and Mossberg inside, then he jumped in and took out his .45 which he used as one lone gunman tried a shot from the first stairwell. Mark returned the fire and felt the chopper lift up and away and out of range.

"Good buddy, we made it!" Mark said.

Ralston didn't say a word.

The Penetrator looked at him and saw that he was holding his hand over the left side of his chest.

"You've been hit," Mark said. He eased the man back and took the controls. "I can fly this thing. Just lean back and take it easy."

Mark worked the controls and found them much like other choppers he had flown. They were high enough over the city now so there were no life-death critical moments on the controls. He made a few small errors in control, but soon felt out the individuality of the craft.

"Hey, Ralston, I've got the ship. Now which way do we go?" Mark asked. But when the Penetrator looked over at the pilot, he saw that Ralston had either died or passed out.

## Chapter 10

## WHAT'S A CRYO????

Mark flew the chopper with one hand and checked Ralston. He was still breathing and had a pulse. Shock must have blacked him out. Now to get the bird and his wounded pilot to the ground. Mark circled, looking for any night lighted runways that would show him where the airport was. He saw them at last, far out to his right and angled that way, wondering if the police would be following him.

By now they should be all over the top two floors of that building. Police and firemen would swarm the place, and there would be very little secret about the headquarters anymore. If any of Preacher Mann's illegal operations were going on there, they would be an open book now that even a bought and paid for police force couldn't ignore.

Police probably also knew about the chopper that made two illegal landings on top of the Home Savings and Loan building. They might try to follow him right now by reports from squad cars around the town. Mark wished he knew the area, then he could pick out a better place to land. Only he had a wounded man on board. There would be good ambulance connections if the cops got to Ralston quickly. Mark headed for the airport, deciding not to land at Ralston's pad, maybe another one. Or he could land on the aircraft taxi strip. That would attract attention and get somebody out there fast. And he would be well away from most of the lights and could fade away in the darkness. Yes, that sounded better. Mark looked at the Mossberg riot gun. There was no time to break it down and stow it in his shoulder bag. He could leave it in the chopper to amuse the cops, or he could dump it in a swamp. He'd take his chances with his own hand hardware, but the long gun would slow down his movements.

Mark had flown the chopper out of the city now and swooped down where he saw moonlight glinting off water. He opened the door flap and jettisoned the Mossberg, watching it splash in the wetness. It wouldn't be found there for a long time. Then he angled for the airport, came in on the back side, hopped over some power lines and landed almost at the end of the turnabout taxi strip. He cut the motors and quickly checked Ralston's pulse, then bailed out, the shoulder bag with the ledgers in it around his neck. He ran hard into the blackness beyond the taxi strip lights and generally toward the chopper pads.

Before he had moved two hundred meters through the darkness he heard sirens and saw flashing lights as three vehicles converged on the chopper which had dropped down without lights and with no radio contact or landing permission. Mark knew that Bud Ralston would get the quickest medical help possible. He

102

stood near the airport fence and watched as flash-
lights probed the bird; then he saw men helping Ralston from the chopper and into an ambulance. It
roared off, siren wailing and lights flashing.

Mark looked at the helicopter pads a half mile
away. Were they covered? Were the police or any of
Preacher's men there? He wished he could simply cut
and run, but he couldn't. His equipment and clothes
were in the Mustang parked at Ralston's pad.

The continuing pain in his shoulder and ribs came
throbbing through again. Mark concentrated on it,
using his psychological powers of *Sho-tu-ça* to block
out the pain and to forget about it until there was
time to take care of it. The Resistweve shirt had probably saved his life tonight. But he was sure that one
or two ribs had cracked and the bruise on his shoulder would be deep and purple for weeks. He beat
down the pain.

As he moved out toward the Ralston helicopter
pad, Mark had eliminated the pain. He utilized the
running pace David Red Eagle had taught him back
at the Stronghold. It was a little faster than a jog,
more like a 5,000 meter, long distance runner's pace.
Mark had conditioned himself so he could run a kilometer at that speed and get there with only a slight
increase in his heart beat and breathing rate, but well
able to go into battle. It had served him well many
times in the past.

Mark reasoned that the sooner he arrived at the
pad and his car, the better. The police would be there
eventually, but now he decided the only ambushers
would be from Preacher Mann's outfit.

The Penetrator came on the chopper area from the
back side, the fence away from the birds, and moved

silently to the corner of building 24A where he looked around from ground height. When he had spoken the sacred words and prayers of *Sho-tu-ça* to help control his bodily pain, he had also summoned up his night vision so he might see as though it were only faintly dusk. It was part psychological and part physical, enabling his eyes to utilize more efficiently the available light. Now he scanned the best hiding spots, and at once found two men. One was not more than twenty feet from him, sitting between the wheels of a tied-down jet helicopter. The other person was farther away, beside a small utility building that sprouted a light pole. This man had a sniper rifle with a night scope on it.

Without a sound and very little open movement, the Penetrator worked his way behind the jet chopper and crawled up to where he could touch the ambusher. From this angle the man could see both Mark's Mustang, two other cars and the door of the Ralston Flying Service. Mark edged closer, drew Ava, and hesitated. The man could be a sheep, not tied in with Preacher Mann. The Penetrator decided it was better to err on the side of caution. He put the death-dart loaded Ava away and brought up his Star .45. Mark waited for a small jet to land and, slammed the heavy automatic down on the man's head. The watcher groaned and slumped, unconscious. After quickly tying the man's hands and feet, Mark faded into the night and came up on the far side of the six-foot-square building by the light pole.

He moved around it slowly, soundlessly, and heard the man on the other side shift positions and hum a tuneless little song. Mark drew Ava again and slid around the corner and faced the ambusher. Quickly

104

Mark recognized the sandy-haired youth who had fingered him the day before.

"Hi, Sandy, you looking for me?"

"How in hell . . . ?" The kid grinned, his hand sliding toward his belt. "Yeah, boss said he wanted to talk with you, so I've been waiting until you got back. None of this snuff jazz. He wants to offer you a job. You're a specialist." As the kid talked, his hand moved under his shirt and he had a weapon half drawn when Mark kicked his hand and set the gun flying.

"You son-of-a-bitch!"

"True, sonny. Las Vegas, the Pink Pussy Casino. It took me a while to remember. You were a 'puller' out on the sidewalk."

"Yeah? So what? You closed it down, burned it up, and you snuffed my boss. So I owe you."

"And you fingered me yesterday when you serviced my plane, but you missed me on the highway and in the ditch. So now you pay for it, sonny."

Mark fired Ava, saw the death dart thud into Sandy's shirt over his heart. The hoodlum shrieked and slumped to the ground, dead in a few seconds. Mark ignored him as he would a swatted fly and checked the grounds again. His night sight showed no one else was hiding, waiting to kill him.

The Penetrator ran to the car, inspected under the hood, then looked on the muffler and tail pipe for any heat-activated bomb. When he was sure the car was clean, he started it and drove away, quietly and without lights along the airport perimeter road until he was well within the commercial passenger section. He parked there and looked over the ledgers he had taken during his whirlwind raid on the Home Savings building. At first nothing made any sense to him.

He turned on the overhead light and went through each book in detail. One was a payroll record, listing names on ledger sheets, showing weekly pay days. The sums seemed small considering what kind of a criminal operation it was. The next ledger was a listing of various operations now in effect, from Mexico brown heroin imports to the call girl trade. The last was a ledger for something called "Operation Cryo." The name made no sense to Mark, who began reading the daily entries. He found payments for everything from seagoing construction cranes to Plexiglas, from plastic tubing to bottles of deuterium and helium-3. None of it made any sense.

The more he read the entries, the more confused he became. Back on the first page was a small explanation but it didn't help much. It said the "Operation Cryo" was started on July 1, and would be ready to go three years hence. It did give the location, Hobe Island, which was shown as being seven miles off the coast of Florida opposite June Beach, which was just up the peninsula a mile or two from West Palm Beach. One entry interested him—"Cryostat," with the prices listed at $24,000 each. The word was on the fringes of his vocabulary, but Mark couldn't bring it to mind.

The list of items purchased was endless—everything from cartons of tooth paste to food and clothing. He checked the first entry and saw it was made three years ago. The total amounts spent were staggering. At the end of one section was a tally sheet that showed from all departments more than three million dollars had been expended so far.

Mark turned on the car's radio and pushed buttons until he found the news. Five minutes after the na-

106

tional news was over the announcer got to the local news.

"Fire, explosions, shootings and we don't know what all, went on late tonight on the tenth floor of the Florida Home Savings and Loan building in downtown West Palm Beach. Firemen now say a two-alarm fire there is under control, but there is heavy smoke damage to the three upper floors. Police and firemen had difficulty even getting to the fire, since there is no direct access by elevators to the top floors. Firemen finally broke down locked doors in the stairs to get to the blaze. Personnel on the site said they had the fire well under control by the time the fire department got to the scene. A top fire department spokesman said that's the usual claim when a company is trying to hide something. He indicated a complete investigation is being made to determine the cause of the blaze and all entries and exits will be carefully examined to be sure that they meet fire code regulations.

"If this outfit is trying to hide something, it won't be hidden anymore," the unidentified fire official said.

"Police report numerous deaths at the site, but they were not revealing the cause of the deaths or giving out numbers or names pending the notification of next of kin. One reporter said he saw at least six bodies in a hallway. He said the dead suffered gunshot and shrapnel wounds. Police would neither confirm or deny the report, but hustled the reporter out of the area and will allow no more 'unauthorized' personnel on the scene until it has been critically examined by the department's police laboratory specialists.

"Police obviously did not want to show what happened. Witnesses say that, just after the smoke erupted out windows on the eleventh floor, a helicopter without lights approached the building. A witness says she thinks the chopper landed on the roof of the Florida Home Savings and Loan building, but she can't say for sure. She assumed that it did.

"From all sketchy reports it seems that the Penetrator has struck again, and that someone or some company on those two top floors was the target. Here is a late report. We now have confirmation on the name of the firm that leases the tenth and eleventh floors. It is the Florida Land and Sea Development Consortium, listed with the state as a holding corporation with ownership of many other firms and businesses, including the Home Savings Building itself."

Mark turned off the radio. There was no way he could get any more details about the hit on the big building. The police had probably swarmed over the place. Preacher Mann himself was undoubtedly gone, if he had been there when it happened. A private elevator to the parking garage in the basement would have moved him out of danger in only seconds.

Where would he go? To his island? How did that chunk of land off the coast fit in? Mark studied the books again. What was going on out there, and why would Preacher Mann spend three million dollars in cold cash?

Mark knew that he had to look into the matter. He wasn't through with Preacher Mann; he had only begun. The island sounded like a strong link in some kind of a crime chain. Tonight would be the ideal time. It was not quite 2:00 A.M. But first he had to make a telephone call. He drove to a phone booth and made three calls before he discovered the right hospital.

"Yes, Mr. Ralston was admitted tonight. Let me give you his floor nurse."

When the next voice came on it was clipped and businesslike.

"Yes, this is floor six, Nurse Jacobson."

"Hi, I'm Bud Ralston's brother in Illinois. Family here is trying to find out how bad hurt Bud is. My sister-in-law called but she didn't know too much herself. How is Bud coming along?"

"We can't give out that information, sir."

"Hey, come on, now. We're family. We want to know if he's critical or dying or what? Should we grab a plane, or is it just a scratch?"

"Well, I guess we should tell you that much. The bullet entered high on the left side of his chest, missing vital organs and lodged in his shoulder. Doctors are removing the bullet now. He lost considerable blood, but there's nothing to indicate he is in any fatal danger. He should be discharged in three or four days with recuperation for another three weeks."

"Hey, that's great. Thanks, nice nurse lady, that's just great. I'll give him a call in a couple of days. Hey, you folks there in Florida are all right people. You're just great. Thanks one whole lot."

"You're welcome, sir."

Mark hung up and got back into his car. The pilot was going to make it. That was good. Mark would get his "wounded in action payment" to Ralston before leaving town.

Now he needed a marina, a good one with some fine boats, but a guard who wasn't quite so fine.

Mark moved out of the phone booth too quickly and the movement felt like somebody hit him in the ribs with a two by four. He gasped and hung onto the door for a minute to let the numbing shock of the sudden pain ebb away. He fought against the pain and, as he did, he reinvested some time in the ancient *Sho-tu-ça* psychological religious rite to drive the pain out of his consciousness.

Five minutes later he was back in the Mustang and driving toward West Palm Beach and the waterfront. A marina—he needed a marina or a yacht club, something substantial but not gaudy. First a check of his available armament. He stopped, brought the suitcase into the front and examined the leftovers. He had a disassembled rifle; a taken-apart M-79 army grenade launcher with twelve rounds that turned it into a small-scale mortar. There was a small assortment of plastic explosives, detonators and fuses, his backup pistols and plenty of spare ammunition. He would be going into an unknown situation, but evidently an installation that had been carefully constructed and stocked. He should be prepared for every eventuality.

## Chapter 11

## ISLAND IN THE ICE

After fifteen minutes of checking the waterfront, Mark found the marina he wanted. This one had a younger guard than most of them. Mark didn't want to risk using a sleep dart on an old man who might not be able to stand the strain of the tranquilizer.

The Penetrator parked the Mustang half a block from the marina and took everything out of it including the two aluminum suitcases. If the island were benign, his equipment and arms would be in no danger. If it were as hot as he figured, he would need all of the weapons and explosives he carried.

Mark walked directly up to the guard at the gate, set down his suitcases and shot a sleep dart into the young man's thick thigh before he could even ask Mark a question. Mark caught the guard, carried him to the little shack and sat him on the chair, then put his folded arms under his head so it looked as though the man were snoozing.

He picked up his bags and hurried down the

floating cement dock looking for just the right boat. He had thought of a sailboat, so he could move in silently and undetected, but there was almost no wind tonight. If the place were important and well equipped, it would have all kinds of electronic detectors functioning anyway.

He looked along the rows of boats until he found what he wanted, a 24-foot Reinell speedboat. She had a planing hull, a little flying bridge, and if she were powered by the same motor as the one he rented in the Bahamas, she could do up to thirty-eight knots in a calm sea. She would do fine. He stepped on board, took off a blue canvas protective cover and stowed his bags, then checked the fuel, over half full, which should be plenty.

It took Mark almost a minute to work with his pics to get the ignition turned on. Then he had the engine started and after a two minute warmup, he chugged away from the marina, down the small arm of water and out through the channel into the blackness of the Atlantic.

Mark powered the little boat north along the coast for what he determined were two miles, then he did a ninety-degree turn to the right, grabbed a compass course due east and held it. He found he could cruise at twenty knots without pounding the little boat too hard. Mark computed the elapsed time to the island. If he didn't see something in twenty minutes, he'd throttle down and have a good look around.

It was almost 3:00 A.M. when Mark cut the engine to a gentle purr. He could see nothing—only the blackness of the Atlantic. The island should be here somewhere. He put the craft on slow throttle and moved ahead for three minutes, then made a ninety-degree turn to the left and held that course for two minutes, then angled due east again.

Mark stared ahead in surprise and cut the engine. He had almost smashed into the black hulk of an island. The Penetrator had expected there would be lights, buildings, fences, searchlights, the works. All he could see was the surf breaking on a small reef outside a gentle cove. The moon wasn't helping much and most of the island was covered with a light fog. The reef protected a small bay no more than fifty feet wide, the back edge heavy with brush and stunted trees. Mark slowly eased the boat around the reef and toward the narrow channel, felt her slide over the submerged rock and then ride into the calm water of the lagoon. He guided the speedboat into an opening in the tangled brush and it slipped in almost out of sight. There he tied it up.

On his way out in the boat, Mark had outfitted himself. He had the M-79 assembled. The army grenade launcher would serve as his artillery and he had slung it over his shoulder on the strap. In the musette shoulder bag he put eight of the special grenade launcher rounds, both high explosive and white phosphorus. He added four half-pound blocks of C-5 plastique explosive along with enough detonators and timers to handle them. Mark took off the wrist knife and, under his tight-fitting Resistweve shirt sleeve, wrapped ten inches of three-inch wide, sheet C-5 plastique. Under that he put a small detonator and timer to give him another surprise explosive package.

Mark had both his .22 High Standard with silencer and his .45 Star automatic in his belt holsters. He had finished assembling his armament with four M-3 fragmentation grenades.

Now, the Penetrator stepped through ankle deep water to the rocky shore and looked over the island. The fog was breaking up as he moved away from the brush and now he could see the dim outlines of the rock pile. It would be a quarter of a kilometer long, not more than one hundred meters wide. In the pale moonlight he could discover no buildings, no indications of any kind that the island was inhabited. But he knew men were here, he could sense it, exactly the same way he had sensed the Viet Cong in Vietnam several years before. He tensed, squatted behind an outcropping of heavy rock and peered over the landscape. The rock shelves rose in a gradual incline for some eighty meters toward the center of the island. Even that high point was not more than twenty meters above sea level. Not much of an island, more like one great big rock. What could Preacher Mann possibly want with it?

Recon? His combat senses told him he should make a soft recon first, but he tempered that urge with a cold reasoning, higher logic. Something was wrong. How could anyone have spent over three million dollars here and not have any sign of it? And where was the security? Hidden security, secret watches and lookouts, perhaps electronic sentries, radar scanners. There had to be some kind of protective devices. Could it have some type of electronic sensors, the electronic "fence" idea? They could be programmed for sound with automatic readouts from a computerized center. Any programmed sounds such as birds and the surf would be ignored, but unprogrammed sounds such as motors, voices, walking, would trigger an immediate response.

Mark moved quietly, wondering if the sound of his

boat's engine at idle had been picked up. If there were sensors it would have definitely been heard. The Penetrator completed his swift movement to a more protected pocket of rock and found it was man made. Splinters and fractures showed where explosives had been used. This was the first evidence Mark had found that indeed there were men at this place.

Without warning the dog came at him from the right, a silent blur of brown hair and flashing white teeth that caught him totally by surprise. He dove backward, pulling out the silenced High Standard. Most guard dogs give a warning to hold, but this one had been trained to attack silently and immediately and to go for the throat. Mark came up to his knees and saw the dog leap at him again. Mark fired three times with the silenced gun and put three rounds into the exposed chest of the German shepherd as it was in the air. The dog crashed against Mark, already dead, his heart penetrated by the .22 slugs.

Mark rolled the dog away and stared around, his night vision now fully activated. But he saw nothing. There was still no sign of man. The dog must have been automatically released from some section underground holding area, then commanded to find and destroy.

It had to be sensors. Mark picked up pieces of shattered rock and threw them as far as he could along the beach into the brush, on the rocks. He threw a dozen of them and then watched the rocky slope critically. If there were sound sensors, the operator would think there was a whole army out there. He threw more to his right and watched the slopes again.

It took place almost too fast for him to see it. A section of rock two feet square slid upward in the face of the slanting island, a brown and black dog surged from the opening and charged toward the surf where the stone had hit. The dog worked the whole area, sniffed, tested the air, whined, and then walked toward Mark's hiding place. It whined again, turned and trotted back to the rock from where it had emerged. Evidently some pressure trigger operated the door which opened and the dog vanished back inside the island.

Why hadn't it come after Mark? The animal had smelled him there, the Penetrator was certain. But some training warned him away, ordered him back to the door. By sector! The dog worked only within his preprogrammed sector! That was very fancy and complicated animal training. Interesting.

To Mark's left a searchlight snapped on. It too must have risen from a recess in the rocks because Mark had not spotted it before. It began a systematic sweep of the area where Mark was, where the dog had not returned. Mark was surprised at the intensity of the light, a million candlepower at least, maybe one of those "stream" lights he had heard about. Blinding. The Penetrator still held the High Standard .22 in his hand. He aimed over the rocks, held the weapon with both hands and fired one shot at the light as it Pivoted almost onto him.

The stream light died.

The blackness that followed was straight from a coal mine at midnight. Mark's eyes adjusted quickly and, with his night vision, he scanned his sector leading up the incline toward the top. Everything seemed to be done by units and sectors, so he'd play along. Directly ahead of him a sheet of the black rock swung sideways. A dim light showed and two infantrymen in full battle dress and arms stormed through the opening and threw themselves flat on the hard rock. They were forty meters away. Mark waited, the High Standard ready. He didn't want to waste his artillery yet. These targets would move closer. They came cautiously, working like trained combat infantrymen, advancing, covering each other, moving in short spurts to avoid aimed shots. Then the lead man made a mistake. He overjudged his next cover and had to belly down in a slight indentation in the rock. Mark sighted in with the deadly .22 and pounded two rounds into the man's neck and chest. He never moved again.

Mark rolled away as soon as he had fired the silenced rounds, and lay flat behind a huge boulder. Suddenly the whole area in which he hid was raked by automatic weapons fire—M-16's, he decided. He wondered what had triggered the barrage. They hadn't heard the silenced High Standard. There could have been some type of electronic equipment on the infantryman that ceased to transmit, identifying the attack. He tried to see from where the firing came, missed most of it, but caught the last burst from the very peak of the small island. There was some kind of concealed firing position commanding the whole island. He hoped they didn't have a deadly .50 caliber machine gun up there.

Mark watched the second infantryman moving toward him. He was less sure now, slower in his dashes. Then the man evidently reached his objective or got new orders via radio, because he moved behind good cover and stayed there. Mark brought up the loaded M-79 grenade launcher. The high point of the mountain was about eighty meters away, easily within the range of the M-79. But what was the target? Mark stared at the top of the hill and the surrounding area, but he could find nothing but rock. A concealed bunker?

He threw stones on both sides of him again, to keep the sensors and operators confused. He was about to begin his movements toward the holed-up man when he saw a thin firing slot open on the crest of the hill. At the same time a powerful loudspeaker came on.

"There is no chance for success in your mission. We have determined how many men are in your landing force. You are completely surrounded. Tell your men to lay down their arms and to assemble at the blue light you now see in front of you. We have pinpointed the locations of each of you invaders by electronic sensors and with infrared and radar scanners. Each man is targeted and locked in to computer-adjusted automatic-firing weapons. If you do not give up within thirty seconds, each designated position will be pulverized by high-velocity rifle and machine-gun fire. Nothing can live through such a barrage."

Mark saw the blue light come on halfway between himself and the island top. He looked down at his weapons which seemed so puny in contrast to the advantage the enemy seemed to have. He shrugged. There was more than one way to get inside a fortress.

## Chapter 12

# CHUTE INTO HELL

Mark was sure the barrage of automatic rifle fire was half bluff and half hope. They couldn't have the whole island zeroed in with firing patterns. Not with all the big boulders, outcroppings of slab rock and depressions where a good infantryman could hide. He sighted in on the top of the hill with the M-79 grenade launcher, adjusted his sighting patterns a little and fired.

The first high-explosive grenade landed short of the hilltop by ten meters, and the blast showered the firing slots with shrapnel. The second round Mark sent up came closer, landing just in front of the firing slots and probably doing more damage.

It also brought return fire from the top of the hill. M-16's, .30 caliber light machine gun and some other weapons laid down a blistering pattern of fire aimed generally at the sectors where Mark lay behind a boulder. He had seen the first weapons open up down the ridgeline and the last at the peak. It continued for perhaps thirty rounds each, then tapered off. When it stopped Mark sighted in with the grenade launcher and fired one more shot at the upper firing slots, then at once he moved, spurting ahead then meters to another pile of big rocks.

He drew no fire, and Mark rose and looked over the rocks. What he saw surprised him. Not more than fifty meters away an eight foot section of the rock rolled back and ten men ran through the opening. The confused men formed up, then began to scatter. But before they moved far Mark dropped a high explosive grenade in the center of them. Three men screamed and fell dead. Two more were wounded. The other five took cover behind rocks. They didn't move, evidently waiting for instructions.

The second round Mark sent in was a W.P. which exploded on top of one of the rocks, spraying the sticky phosphorous in all directions. Two of the soldiers jumped up screaming and ran for the access door, which had closed. They pounded on the rock but it didn't open. At last they fell screaming and then moved no more. One more round of H.E. landed near the troops and convinced the remaining three that they should regroup and seek protection of the magic rock wall door. They vanished a minute later and Mark made another move toward the top of the hill, charging along a small gully for twenty meters to a jumble of rocks. A pair of flood lights came on, bathing the top of the hill and down the near ridge with brilliance. Mark was pinned down. He couldn't move without going into the light.

Ten meters below the top of the hill a new threat lifted through a trap door. It was a mounted .50 caliber machine gun, complete with gunner at the double handles. As soon as it came to position, the gunner slammed round after round at the rocks where Mark had taken refuge. The half-inch thick slugs pounded the rocks and screamed away. Mark quickly loaded another H.E. round and fired, half blind. He missed. The next shot he held until there was a momentary lull in the machine gun's chatter. It struck the .50 caliber machine gun base mount, blowing the gunner off his feet and ruining the bolt, putting the gun out of action.

Suddenly all the lights snapped off, dropping the area into inky blackness.

Mark grabbed the M-79 and dashed to his next preselected cover, one huge boulder that rose ten feet out of the rock slab. He checked for the dogs. Now Mark was in a new sector, the one where the dog had looked and given up. However the animal didn't come out. This would be considered a combat operation and the dogs evidently were not used at these times. The Penetrator moved his concentration to the top of the hill. He saw no activity. His night vision came back after the blinding light was extinguished, and now he saw that even the firing slots were closed. The machine gun had been drawn back into its cave.

What would they try next? Mark guessed that this was the first combat experience for the island. It had been given an elaborate system of security, the men had been trained and rehearsed, but that was nothing like the real thing. They certainly were not used to absorbing casualties, or to taking return fire. As he waited he stared at the crest of the hill. There now appeared to be some kind of an opening or wall, perhaps to shield a doorway or tunnel. Anything here should be well made, permanent.

Mark was getting ready to make another surge toward the top when the loudspeaker came on again.

"This is a final warning to the attacking force. Your group is simply too small to challenge us. We can put out a large security force, suffer casualties and drive you into the sea. However it has been decided to function another way. There is no chance you can harm us. We are buttoned up and sealed in here. We have no desire to kill all of you, but if that is what it takes, we will not shrink from that course.

"Therefore you have five minutes to exfiltrate from this island. That should be adequate time. At the end of that grace period we will release from preprogrammed outlets all over the surface of the island, a heavy, colorless and odorless gas which we have developed called methocyanchloride. Every person, all animal life on the surface of this island and on the surrounding water will die in fifteen seconds after breathing the gas. This nerve gas acts so quickly there is no chance to escape it once it has been released. After twenty-four hours it is absorbed by the moisture-laden sea air and broken down into harmless compounds. So, remember, you have only five minutes to leave the island. After that you will be in mortal danger."

Mark looked over the land mass and shook his head. It was a bluff, pure and simple. There was no way they could blanket the island with anything except natural fog. A light breeze had sprung up and blew in from the far side of the island. Gas just wouldn't work. He had never heard of any gas called methocyanchloride, but anything with chlorine in it had to be dangerous. Was it made up of methane, cyanide, and chlorine? Impossible.

Mark threw stones, rocks and boulders again, pitching them as far as the could to excite the sensors. Then he made another dash toward the top of the mountain. He watched every rock in front of him. None opened to discharge troops, dogs, or gas. The Penetrator was within ten meters of the top now, behind a low ridge of rock. He breathed deeply and waited. The five minutes would be over soon.

The loudspeaker came on once more. "One minute and counting. You should be in or near your boats at this time ready to clear the death zone. Please move promptly."

Mark threw more rocks, wondering if it did any good.

"Time," the loudspeaker voice boomed. "A few seconds grace to inform you that if you are a landing party from the Department of Justice, we will give you increased reasons for leaving. We have captured one of your agents, a J-6 named Joanna Tabler. She is unharmed and here on the island, and will be executed at once if the attacking force is not pulled back. If you can still hear my voice you soon will be in deadly peril."

Joanna! Mark thought. So they did get her and had brought her to the island sometime yesterday. Then she was not at the headquarters earlier tonight when he had searched for her. He watched for some evidence of a gas being dispersed, saw none and made another dash for the hilltop. Mark's foot hit a trip wire. He recognized what it was, falling to the rocks at once, hoping to lessen the chances of being hit by shrapnel from the antipersonnel mine. But it was not a mine, it was only a flare that shot a hundred feet into the air and exploded with a blinding light, drifting silently away on a small parachute. Mark jumped up and continued his run the last dozen meters to the top, working from his musette bag a square of plastique, and timer-detonator as he ran.

Mark slammed to the ground at the very top of the hill. There was only a shelf of rock where the firing slits had been and now a blank wall that held a camouflaged door. It had no handle but the rough opening was plain. Mark forced part of the C-5 under the crack at the bottom of the panel and plastered the rest against the door. It took him a few seconds to set the timer-detonator, being sure he turned it to twenty seconds, not twenty minutes. He activated it and rushed around the rocky corner of the wall holding both hands over his ears.

The explosion was sharper than he expected, exchoing off the rocky sides of the wall. When he charged around the corner, he found a hole where the hidden door had been. The door had splintered and blasted inward, showering a rough-hewn tunnel with shards of wood and stone. Mark saw no one in the tunnel and, with one gun in each hand, he moved in ready to fire. His special night vision told him the tunnel ran slightly downward, conforming to the angle of the outside land mass. After twenty feet there was another door, this one with rugged metal hinges and a complicated locking device.

Mark ran to the door, working on another charge. Without wasting time or motions, he put the timer for thirty seconds and after activating it, ran out of the tunnel to get away from the blast.

Twin explosions came right on schedule, and Mark felt the whole top of the mountain jolt from the shock waves. Inside he found the six-inch-wide metal door blown off its hinges, hanging to one side so he could pass through. Before he charged into an unknown and hostile area, Mark examined it. There were electric lights on the far side of the door. They had not been broken by the blast which punched most of its fury into the steel on this side.

Inside the corridor the floor was finished in some type of shiny black tile, the walls plastered and the ceiling covered with hardboard and painted. Mark threw a chunk of metal on the gleaming floor, but it only skidded along a dozen feet and did not set off any charge or make an electrical connection. The floor was not electrified.

Mark moved along the polished floor quickly, yet with caution. Somehow this was too easy. Where were the men with the M-16s? Surely the sensors showed the blasting of the two doors. They had to know someone was inside. Why didn't they respond? Or were they sucking him into a trap where he couldn't get out?

He reached into his shoulder bag and pulled out an M-3 fragger and held it. He zipped up the bag and looped it over his head, then slung it around to his back with the M-79 to give him more freedom of movement.

Ahead Mark saw another door. This one did not look like a security panel—in fact it stood slightly ajar. He walked faster, wondering where they had Joanna, what they were doing to her.

The floor looked as shiny and black as the rest of it, but when he was near the far end, only a dozen feet from the open door, a ten foot section fell away under him and dropped him downward. With the first surprise his hands went up and the High Standard auto-

125

matic flew from his left hand. He reached for the surface of the floor but it was too slick to get a grip on. Then he was gone, thumping into a metal funnel that quickly narrowed into a chute of some kind, spinning him downward at a sixty-degree angle. There was nothing to catch or grab. The inside of the chute was as slippery as a waxed con man.

With a reflex action Mark clasped his arms to his chest to hold on to the shoulder bag and the M-79. As he fell through the darkness he realized he still held the M-3 fragger in his hand.

Then his feet hit water. He gulped in what he figured might be his last breath of air just before the water closed around him and the shoulder bag streamed out above him as he struggled to hold on to it.

Gradually the downward plunge into the water slowed and when he looked up he could see light. Mark used both hands and stroked for the surface, kicking furiously. He still had the grenade in his hand. He reached over and pulled out the pin of the small bomb, holding the handle tightly so it wouldn't go off, but it would be ready. Mark kicked for the surface. Just before his last bit of reserve breath bubbled out of his mouth, he broke through to the light and air and gulped in a huge breath.

As he came out of the water he saw he was in a cavern with a dome-shaped top, an underwater pool of some sort in a natural cave. Then he fell back under water. Straight ahead and below, he saw the most frightening sight of his life. A thirty-foot great white shark surged upward at him, its huge jaws open, a glint of hunger and fury in its cold fish eyes.

## Chapter 13

## SHARKS! SHARKS!

Mark had time only to jerk the M-79 off his shoulder and ram it sideways across the rows of huge teeth in the shark's mouth as it came at him. Then he pushed the live grenade into the gaping mouth just as the shark swerved, evidently distracted by the sudden attack and the object in its jaws.

The unusual offensive action caused the shark to alter its course at the last moment. It surged past Mark and out of the water in a typical great white shark attack. It crashed back into the water a dozen feet away, four seconds later, and the hand grenade detonated, sending fifty shards of hot metal into the animal's head and body. Mark made sure to keep his head out of the water when the bomb went off. He saw the shark shudder, flip over and try to swim away, but too many nerve endings had no motor sensors. The huge fish spun in a lazy circle and began sinking.

Mark churned the water as he swam a dozen feet

to a shelf of rock and scrambled out of the pool as he saw half a dozen other sharks gliding into his side of the chamber. He lay on the ledge panting, and saw the smaller sharks nudge the thrashing form of the great white. Then as blood stained the water, one shark drove in and took a mouthful of flesh off the big predator. Soon eight or ten sharks of many types were tearing into the flesh of their former master, ripping it apart with sharp teeth, tearing the thirty-foot-long fish into bloody ribbons until the whole pool looked like one big slaughterhouse. Mark lay quietly watching the savage end of the big animal.

He took inventory of his armament. The .45 Star automatic still lay in its tuck-in holster on his belt. It would function well despite the swim. He drained out his shoulder bag and found the remaining explosives wet but intact, and the timer-detonators all ready to go. There were two more fraggers he'd saved, and two rounds for the M-79 which he flipped into the pool. His small arms supply would have to be enough.

Mark peered over the top of the ledge and stared at the underseas grotto. It was a natural, sculptured cave, with the water level evidently dependent on the tides. It could have been carved out by wave action thousands of years ago or been formed by a gaseous pocket when the land lifted from the waters. Blue-black rock formed the walls and now he saw that nearby a walkway had been cut all around the pool. Evidently there was only one way out.

As Mark watched he saw someone come through the far door. The man wore an Eskimo-type fur parka and walked to the edge of the pool staring with surprise at the activity below. As he watched the feeding sharks, Mark edged around behind him and came to within six feet before the man heard him. He spun around, but already Mark had covered the remaining ground and caught the man in the pit of his stomach with a crashing right fist which doubled over the fur parka. The Penetrator's knee jolted upward, connecting with the man's face, tumbling him backward and dropping him into the shark pool. The man had time to scream only once before a hammerhead shark slammed into him, biting off his head in one gulp. The wide-nosed shark turned at once for a second helping.

Ahead twenty feet, Mark saw the door. He ran to it, eased it open slowly, and found a hallway that seemed like it came out of any business building or research center. It was shiny white—floor, walls and ceiling. Doors showed on both sides, but after a dozen they gave way to glassed-in cubicles from four to six feet square and eight feet high. Each had a separate door; all were empty.

Mark saw no one, heard no music, or voices. But then it was after 3:20 A.M. The Penetrator moved down the corridor farther and found more of the glass boxes, but now some of them showed frost inside. The floor slanted downward again, then leveled off.

Here the glassed-in squares were larger and he stopped in amazement when he spotted a German shepherd dog, standing in the center of one of the cells. The dog was frozen stiff!

Now each of the rooms contained an animal, some standing, some lying in a corner—All kinds of animals—cats, a donkey, a pony, even one full-sized horse, and all completely frozen.

The Penetrator tried to give it a purpose. Surely not

food storage. That industry was much more advanced than this. This was freezing the whole animal.

Cryo. . . .

The word kept coming back to him. Cryo, it was on the ledger book, but where had he heard it before? Then he knew—cryogenics—the whole word meant very low temperatures. Cryogenics was used in many fields today from lowering bodily temperature before an operation to the frozen food industry to cryosurgery to something wild called cryobiology he had heard about which studied the effects of extremely low temperatures on the whole biological system. Somewhere he remembered that, by taking an organism down to absolute zero, all biological activity, including growth and deterioration could be halted.

But why a whole animal here?

Mark heard voices down the corridor. He moved into a windowed office and turned his back as the group went by. They wheeled a hospital gurney on which lay a body draped by a sheet.

"I don't care what you say," a heavily accented voice insisted. "I still hold that it's a new anticoagulant we need. This heparin may not be the right type. There should be others we can choose from. We'll find out for sure on this one."

"The blood plasma was not right," another voice said. "We had it working and then they said to use DMSO. Is anyone really running this program or is it just a mish-mash?"

The four went on by, wheeled the gurney into one of the chilled cubicles and soon came back with the empty cart. When they had gone Mark went to the glass and checked. The body was that of a young gorilla, no bigger than a child. It lay on a table, evidently frozen solid.

When the Penetrator turned around he came face to face with a man in his thirties wearing a white medical coat and with fury in his eyes.

"What the hell are you doing in here? This is restricted to class one medical only. You should know that."

Mark shrugged. "Well, I do, but you know, I was curious." In one swift motion the Penetrator grabbed the medic around the neck with his arm, putting pressure on both carotid arteries leading up either side of his throat. Mark bent to one side, lifting the doctor off his feet and the medic's face turned purple as he struggled, then he sighed and went limp. Mark had "choked him out" as so many police would do with unruly people during arrests. It would present no lasting damage and the victim would wake within two or three minutes.

Mark dragged the man into the office he had just left, closed the door and knelt down on the floor below the window level. He went through the man's pockets, found only a badge with picture I.D. and some magnetic codings that Mark couldn't understand, or duplicate. He tied the man with some of his ever-present monofilament fishing line, fifteen-pound weight, took the I.D. card, then went back into the hall.

At the next cross corridor, Mark found more of the glass-enclosed cold boxes. He saw the end of the hall and ran for it. There was a door there, and it was not locked. Steps led downward. As soon as Mark started down, he saw he was off the medical floor and into nuts and bolts. Huge machines loaded with pipes, tubes and ducts of all kinds filled the area. Mark landed on the bottom and turned toward the machinery.

He almost missed the attack. A young man jumped out from a blind corner and swung a 12-inch crescent wrench at Mark's head.

Only his highly trained reflexes helped Mark dodge the wicked blow. He caught the wrench in one hand and grabbed the man's oil-stained shirt with the other.

"Damnit, damnit, damnit!" the youth wailed. "My one chance and I blow it. Goddamnit to hell!"

"Your one chance to what?" Mark asked sternly.

"To get out of this hell hole! I signed up to work on refrigeration equipment through an ad. They made damn sure I was qualified and checked out. Then I get here and you guys won't let me go."

"Won't let you go?"

"Hell no. I can't swim seven miles, can you?" He frowned. "Hey, who the hell are you. You ·ain't no doctor."

"I'm the guy who came to get you out of this hell hole. And I'm not one of them. I'm one of you. What can you tell me about this place? What do they do here? What's going on?"

"Damned if I know. They tell me to keep the iron working, so I keep it running. Twenty-four hours a day I keep it running. You know they have more cooling capacity here than for the Empire State Building? Some of them damned cells upstairs go down to absolute zero. That's a minus four-hundred and sixty degrees Fahrenheit below zero!"

"Everyone up there scientists?"

"I don't know, maybe crazy professors, I don't

know. I had to go upstairs and fix a leak in this one place, and on the table they've got this beautiful young girl. She's tied down and just as naked as the day she was whelped. A real knockout. They actually killed her, right there while everyone watched. They shut off her oxygen and then, when she was dead, they hooked her up to a heart and lung machine and all sorts of gadgets and needles and jazz, and then they had me start to bring down the temperature in the room. Gradual, they said, and before they were done, that knockout of a girl was frozen stiff as an icicle on a barn roof in the middle of winter."

"The animals, the frozen animals. What are they for?"

"Experiments, I guess. Near as I can figure out they been at it for over a year now, trying to get everything just right. Now, I'm not saying why, but those kooks are trying to freeze animals whole and then bring them back to life. So help me, I saw them trying it once. Didn't work. I don't want to know no more than that, I just want out of this crazy place."

Mark had long since let go of the young man and given him back his wrench.

"I want you out of here, too. Now what can you tell me about the layout of the rooms upstairs?"

"Nothing. They blindfolded me each time I went up there. I don't know what the next floor is like at all. This is the bottom one, I know that."

"Then I'll have to find out myself." Mark looked at his watch. The waterproof—everything proof—model was still running. "It's 3:25 A.M. now. See how much of a snarl you can make in the refrigeration mechanics so half of the units will blow out at exactly 4:00 A.M. Can you arrange that?"

"Yeah, sure, but they'll beat me up. They done it before."

"Not this time. I'm planning on blowing up this whole devil's paradise before sunup today. Can you help me?"

"Hell, why not? This is the creepiest goddamn place I've ever been. They can keep their high pay."

"Remember, 4:00 A.M. Now I'd better get back upstairs and try to find something else that's vital. Know where the power plant is?"

The kid shook his head.

Mark retraced his steps, got to the next floor and scanned the hallway. It was clear of people. He moved out along the main corridor. Mark had nothing to hide now. He walked down the center of the hall, putting together a quarter pound plastique bomb as he went. When it was ready he pressed it against one of the freeze cells, set the timer-detonator for thirty seconds and hurried away from it. He had just passed another cross corridor when the bomb went off. The lights dimmed for a second, then he heard a wailing siren, and people rushed from everywhere. They ignored Mark. He walked past them, and soon he was away from most of the people. The corridor changed now and became a carpeted floor with oil paintings on the paneled walls. Ahead another fifteen feet he came to a reception desk with a well-groomed young man behind it. He looked up.

"Yes, sir, we've been instructed to ask you to wait here for your guide. You are our visitor from Cuba, aren't you? Mr. Voightlander will be here in just a moment."

Mark looked at the receptionist and kept walking. He barely passed the desk when the young man rose with a .38 revolver in his hand and pointed it at Mark.

"I'm really going to have to insist that you wait for your escort."

Behind him Mark saw two guards in uniform come from a room. Each one had an automatic shotgun with a shortened barrel. Mark was sure each weapon held five to eight rounds.

The Penetrator's law: Never argue with a loaded shotgun especially when it's pointed directly at you.

"Well, why not?" Mark said. "I might as well wait and see what Mr. Voightlander can do for me."

## Chapter 14

## THE GUIDED TOUR

Voightlander came a moment later, talked with the guards at the desk, then motioned for Mark to move ahead of him.

"So you're the fly in our ointment? Frankly I had expected something bigger, better, tougher." A door opened and Mark was motioned through it.

"Inside, tough guy killer, we want to have a short talk with you," Voightlander said.

Mark watched for his chance, but the guards stayed well back. When they were in the room, one guard kept Mark under a big gun while the other moved in close and put his shotgun at Mark's throat. The first guard searched Mark, took the .45 and musette bag, but found nothing else. All Mark had left was the plastique around his forearm and the surprises in his belt. To his amazement they did not take his belt.

Voightlander, a small man with a brush "flat top"

haircut and snapping black eyes approached Mark and slapped his face. Mark did not react.

"You swine! You filthy pig! You blast your way inside here and kill one of my men, then blow up a dozen of our cryonic retaining cells. You are worse than dead! Put your hands behind you at once!"

Mark reacted slowly and had them jerked back by a guard, then felt steel handcuffs snapped on. They were tightened too much on purpose.

"Now, you are properly prepared to go see your master, the man who even now controls your destiny, your life. But that isn't going to last long, so don't worry about it. Move!"

Mark felt a shotgun jab in the back and he walked where they pointed him. They carefully stayed away from him so the scatter guns could not miss. The cuffs worried him. He was no quick escape artist. Mark could get out of them with time, but he was sure there was not much of that around. He wanted to get to the absolute guts of this operation, and this was as good a way as any he knew.

They were down a corridor, past a kitchen, then to another area and into a luxurious apartment, with murals on the walls, spacious rooms with indirect lighting, thick carpet, large TV set on the wall and sitting at a free form desk a huge man who could only be Preacher Mann.

The big black rose as Mark came into the room. The shotgun guards moved to either side, covering Mark, yet keeping their leader off the firing pattern. Someone hit Mark in the back of the knees, forcing him to kneel. The Preacher loomed over him. One big hand came from the right and then from the left, swatting Mark's face as though it were a fly, rocking it from side to side.

The Penetrator's senses tumbled for a moment, then steadied and he looked up at the man.

"Runt! You are nothing but an insignificant, undersized, overpublicized ordinary man. I thought you must be twenty feet tall, with thunderbolts in your hands. So you are the mighty Penetrator? It doesn't look like you could hurt a half-grown midget with an inferiority complex."

The man's black eyes stared into Mark's. Preacher Mann was indeed shaved bald, with a massive full black beard six inches long. He rubbed the moustache out of his mouth, preening it back.

"You realize, insignificant vertebrate, that you have done me a great injustice. Your attack on my downtown headquarters was most inopportune, destructive, embarrassing, and totally unwarranted. What did it net you in results? One ledger perhaps that gave you enough information about this island to make you curious."

Preacher Mann slapped Mark again, but gently this time.

He stepped back and strode around the room.

"My illustrious captive. You have little idea how much joy this gives me. Just to know that you are in my power. Oh, power is no stranger to me. I know full well that power has the ability to corrupt, as William Pitt said in old England. And as someone else said, absolute power will corrupt absolutely. However I have many acquaintances around the country who will heap gold and riches and plaudits on me for bringing about your sudden demise."

Mark sensed no one near him, and sprang to his

139

feet. Evidently someone behind him moved, but Preacher gave a curt signal with one hand and Mark was not forced back down.

"Spirit, yes, I've heard that you have spirit. The one man who identified you so readily also had spirit, but he was foolish and unwise and greedy. Now, of course, dead. Do not have that much hope, Penetrator, because I have not made up my mind what I shall do with you: Keep you as a toy? Send your head to some New York Italian businessmen I know? Hire you on as my own private expert?"

The big man returned to his chair, a huge leather executive type with high back. He swung around holding an exact copy of a Kentucky flintlock black powder pistol in his hand, the .44 muzzle pointing directly at the Penetrator.

"One of my hobbies is black powder shooting. Now, Mr. Penetrator, evaluate your operation here so far. Critique yourself, your functioning. Criticism is good for everyone. Tell me where I went wrong, and then how you failed. Especially I want to know how you got through the shark tank. It had to be a total surprise to you. There was no way you could have known it was there. My TV cameras, which followed you since you came through the first tunnel door, did not show me how you destroyed the fiercest of all the man-eating sharks."

Mark had long before decided to play a role conflicting with Preacher Mann. He would be as low-caste, foul-mouthed and hoodlum-stupid as the Preacher was trying to be refined.

"You sonofabitch! What the hell you talking like some damned college professor for? You a Harlem nigger who don't know his place? What the fuck you trying to do, nigger, freezing all the white chicks? You nuts or something?"

The black man stared at Mark for twenty seconds and the Penetrator thought he might have pushed too far. Then the big man chuckled, and laughed and at last guffawed in true humor. He wiped tears from his eyes and shook his head in amazement.

"You are an original, one of a kind, Penetrator. You come on rough and crude, trying to get me angry. What was I supposed to do, something stupid so you could get away? That kind of a tactic won't work. I've been baited by experts. Besides, I've outgrown anger. An intelligent man must use his brain, not his emotions to get anywhere. The lesser animals and the lesser humans let anger, fear and violence control their lives. That's why they are lower on the scale than the rest of us."

"Now, we were talking about your escape from the pool. How did you do it?"

"The handcuffs—take them off first," Mark said with no emotion.

"Yes, of course, my apologies. Some of my men are still rather fear oriented." He nodded at once of the guards who unlocked the steel cuffs and Mark rubbed his wrists.

"The shark was easy. The great white is sensitive around the jaws and teeth. I jammed an M-79 grenade launcher in his mouth crosswise and then threw in an army fragmentation hand grenade. The rest of the sharks finished the job."

"Ingenious, and lucky. Now enough of the formalities. You may be aware that I have productive operations going in this area in a number of different fields. I'm always on the watch for extraordinary men.

141

You certainly qualify. I'd like to put you on my staff, hire your expertise, and eventually win your loyalty."

"As an executioner?"

"That's a bit crude for a job description, but an employer can't have everything. If the occasion demands you might have some of that work, but there is so much else for you to do. Take our current project. Actually on this island we are ten to fifteen years ahead of the general state of the art of cryobiology. We have made breakthroughs you wouldn't believe. Do you know that we have frozen a dog and brought him back to life? True. Only the smallest mistake or it would have been perfect. We had slightly too many intercellular collapses, but now we have developed what we think is the solution."

"Those were some of the animals I saw frozen?"

"Yes, some of our failures, our mistakes, some of the experiments from which we have learned much. When we discover how not to do it, we have learned something—that's progress. But now we have a real breakthrough. I was talking with our Dr. Lautherine this morning. He has discovered that, when certain fish feel the water around them getting colder, they produce automatically in their systems a special fluid that in effect acts exactly like antifreeze in your car radiator. The cooler it gets, the more antifreeze is produced and the fish swim around normally. At the point where the water becomes ice, the fish have so much antifreeze in their systems that they are frozen into slush, yet they are still alive. Dr. Lautherine says he has discovered the chemical compound the fish use for their antifreeze. Now we are synthesizing that and adapting it to the systems of animals and to humanoids. Now isn't that a startling discovery!"

"Not if it kills the host. You've been experimenting with live humans?"

"In the interests of science, we have made some tests. Naturally we can't always guarantee results in the beginning. Man has thirsted after eternal life for centuries. This may be the best bet yet. You of course know about Professor Robert Ettinger's book, *Prospect of Immortality, Now,* in 1962. The Life Extension Society has for years tried to do what we have done: freeze the just dead or near dead, with the hopes of bringing them back to life when cures for diseases and medical science advances so they then can have normal and full lives. Unfortunately they were and still are far from being totally scientific about it, and the structural cell damage from freezing has been massive. Am I boring you?"

"No. But I was wondering just where you get your scientific subjects. Hardly volunteers. I've seen reports of beautiful women missing from several sections of the country. Are you preparing a stable of beautiful people for your holding cells?"

"Not at the moment, but I do have an interest in beauty. And I have a continuing need for such females. But we're still too premature to risk anything here which is so valuable to us on the open market. We're in the middle of probably the most difficult of all problems. The worst freezing injury to a human occurs when the protein molecules within the cells collapse due to dehydration. As you can understand, the effect of such denaturing to the brain is devastating. The revived physical body would be perfect, but the mind would have gone and we'd have an idiot or worse, which would not suit our purposes at all."

Mark had been weighing the chances of escape.

143

They were less than zero from this room. He had to wait.

"I still maintain when you're dead, you're dead," Mark said. "It's one big long sleep and your freezing isn't going to help."

"I wouldn't argue with that for a moment, sir. What I'm trying to do is stretch out that active life into a longer time slot, give the body a rest through a cryogenic sleep instead of your death sleep."

"I'll believe it works when I see it."

"Quite right, sir, the pragmatist. That's my cue to begin to be a more proper host and show you around my cozy little establishment. By the way, you do know we could have killed you at any time after you blasted through the first door. You were under constant video observation all the way to the chute, and then again in the pool and through your wanderings in the corridors. We only lost you once for a short span of time. You do fascinate me, and I could use your talents, so let me convince you with a guided tour."

They left by another door and soon were in a hospitallike operating room. Several medical machines stood by, a white-gowned team of men watched a young girl lying on a table. She was nude, pretty and evidently frozen. All the men in the room wore heavy clothing.

"In this test case, the subject has been prepared according to our latest and best scientific data. Her body was perfused directly after her death by a new combination of the antifreeze solution and plasma. I'm sorry, but I can't pronounce the name of the compound. This is said to condition the body cells and prevent the collapse of the protein in the molecules

144

within the the cells. My scientists tell me there will be no collapse whatsoever due to the cell's retention of a greater amount of the antifreeze liquid in the protein, so it won't dehydrate, and can't collapse."

Mark felt an unreasoning rage building within him. How could this maniac talk this way about a human being! One he had probably killed so he could experiment on her! Mark tempered his rage, refining and converting it into potent mental and physical energy that he could use later.

"This chamber is warmed at the rate of two degrees an hour for as long as the mass of the subject requires. But at this point the warming is speeded up so the outer areas of the body will not become warmed and degenerated from lack of circulation before the heavier sections of the subject are fluid again and pliable. I'm sure you recognize the various equipment. It will begin functioning at the moment it is possible to pump the subject's perfused blood and plasma through her veins. It should happen shortly."

Mark watched with a tempered fury. The girl must have been about twenty, long blond hair, cute face with a pointed little nose and an exquisite, well-formed body.

A readout on the wall over them showed her body temperature. Preacher Mann paced back and forth. The guards kept Mark well covered in their sights at all times.

The Bennett Pasitine Pressure machine started automatically. It ran for thirty seconds, then shut down. It could not circulate the air through the lungs. Another two minutes and the machine came on again. The men had now taken off their outer heavy coats. The temperature of the chamber was 98.6 degrees, an

145

artificial womb. This time the machine kept pumping. Another device circulated the blood through the once-frozen girl. One doctor peered into the girl's eye with a special instrument. The pupil did not contract. The heart was being forced to function, the blood was making it work, the lungs were being forced to aerate the blood. Above, by the temperature chart, was a large readout for a sensitive brain-wave meter. The scientists looked at it constantly, but the needle never moved. There was no readout action from her brain waves at all. They continued to check.

The medical man in charge brought in an electric shock machine and placed the electrodes on her chest. The lung machine was shut off and the electric shock jolted her body. There was no reaction. Again, then three times, the heart was given the electrical stimulus, but it would not start pumping on its own. The lung machine was turned on again and it continued to force air through her lungs. Still there was no readout on the brain wave dial.

A sweating doctor took off his mask and picked up a microphone which was connected to the hall loudspeaker system.

"I'm sorry, sir, there has been a malfunction, a mistake somewhere. Our best procedures were all followed religiously in the perfusion of the new fluid, the chilling and the thawing. However we cannot induce the heart to function by itself, nor the lungs. We have absolutely negative readings from the brainwave indicators. The subject is dead."

Preacher Mann shrugged, and led Mark down the hall.

"We are progressing. Each time we get a little closer. We shall find the clue yet. For now it is work,

work, work. If this subject did not revive, the scientists have elected to go with a somewhat older one, a more mature person who we think may have less tendency to dehydrate, which almost everyone agrees now is the key to the successful freeze/thaw syndrome."

Preacher walked in a door and looked to see that Mark followed him. The room was small with a curtain across the far side. When Mark and the two shotgun guards were inside, Preacher smiled at Mark.

"Here is our next subject we think is about perfect. She's a little older and an ideal test case. What do you think, Mr. Penetrator?"

The curtain swept apart. In a chair beyond the one-way glass sat a very much alive and naked Joanna Tabler.

## Chapter 15

## KENDO SLAUGHTERHOUSE ONE

It took every muscle in Mark's body at maximum strain pressure not to react. His eyes remained passive, not a twitch, not a tightening, not a glimmer of recognition. The big black man watched Mark critically, and when the shock value of it had passed, Mark let a broad grin spread over his face.

"One thing about you, Preacher, you sure know how to pick pretty women. And the way you dress them ain't bad neither!"

"She's nothing outstanding, but this one has been troublesome, so we'll use her as a test case. She works for a man in the Justice Department called Dan Griggs. Ever heard of him?"

Mark had been ready for that one and shook his head easily, giving no sign of surprise.

"Preacher, I'm not much of an organization man, know what I mean? I like to go my own way, and plenty of cops are on my tail to make sure I keep going. What's this Justice Department jazz? I thought they ran the border inspection places."

"Right, Mr. Penetrator. And since you're not working with them, or the cops, why not throw in with me for a while? I go my own way too, and can always use a top hand."

"I like your broads, got any more?"

"Dozens, come look over my stable."

They went out the door and down the corridor fifty feet to a big room with a glass window fronting it. It was a large lounge and recreation room. Inside were ten women in various costumes. All were sleek, well-groomed, and beautiful.

"Now this is my test treasure chest, Penetrator. All of these girls I can sell on the world market to the right-minded sexy tycoon. I deliver by private jet, any shape, size, color, and rental is strictly by the hour, portal to portal. My service is the best, but since I offer such variety, I have personnel problems. The girls get tired, they get sick, or worst of all they get fat and I'm stuck with distressed merchandise."

He waved his hand down the corridor. "That's why I'm pushing my cryobiologists. When they get through with all their scientific mumbo-jumbo and perfect the system, it will be fool proof. Freeze the girls now, thaw them lated to fill an order. Ship to China, England, the Sudan, Borneo, Argentina. Bring them back and refreeze until that make and model is needed again. It's a procurer's dream."

Mark had taken the shock of the man's words without any visual change, but inside he was seething. The man was callous, inhuman. How could he plan such a thing? Mark knew he should make some comment.

"Yeah, it might work. Don't know if I'd like a quick thaw broad or not, I mean, she wouldn't be the same." Mark could find no flaw in the guards' work, their positions or movements. They had him perfectly targeted at all times. They were professionals. He had to work another gambit for escape. "So you got the dames, that I don't mind one way or the other. But you go for the hard stuff, too. I don't go for the horse and coke and all that hard death. I don't dig it. So no way could I work for you."

"Come on, now, my good man. There are many fringe benefits, like a free hand with the female merchandise, world-wide travel—many, many benefits."

"And maybe I still end up shark bait. I hear you stay in shape, that right, fatso?"

Preacher Mann laughed. "There you go again, underestimating me. I know I'm not fat, and wouldn't care if I were. But don't try to get me angry that way. It's useless. If you're saying that you think you can beat me one-on-one, say so. I don't know what sport or combat it might be. I'm clearly the stronger, larger, heavier. What could you excel in over me?"

"Anything. Name it, I'll try it. How about .45 automatics at fifty feet?"

Preacher Mann roared with laughter, his huge frame shaking with glee. "You break me up, little man. Always with a funny line. Now if you had said sabers, or ball and mace or even karate, I might have found it more realistic."

"You've been in Cuba and South America. How about fighting staves, quarter staffs."

"Penetrator, you can't be serious. I'm an expert with the quarter staff. You couldn't stay two minutes with me."

"Try me then. What do you have to lose? You put me down without killing me and I'll consider joining your outfit. Only no work with the damn dopers."

The big black man frowned. "You must have some ulterior motive in mind, but for the life of me I can't determine what it might be. Why not? It should be most amusing. I haven't had my workout yet this early A.M. Your arrival disturbed my sleep, but I should be able to finish you in two minutes, then I can get back to my bed. I have two charming Chinese girls waiting for me there."

Mark wondered why the big man had consented so quickly. Had it been a mistake? He was right on one point: there was no use in trying to out-psych Preacher to make him angry. The man simply didn't function that way. He was Mr. Spock-logic-oriented all the way. Mark was relying on his mastery of the Oriental martial arts and the kendo techniques with the quarter staff. He could use it to fight with much like he would a samurai sword, and he would have less trouble with the bulk and weight of the big man. It was an agility and reaction game.

The only problem was that Mark could not win too quickly over the crime lord. And what would be in the fighting arena with them? An audience, or only the shotgun guards? Who else might be there?

The Preacher led the way around the corner to a small gymnasium. He told Mark he had built it for himself and for the girls to work out in so they would stay in shape. A large section was cleared and quarter staffs presented. These training staffs were real ones. made not of doweling, but from some hard South African tree limbs over four feet long, as straight as rulers, and an inch thick. One swipe with the stick

152

could break an arm, pulverize a spinal column or break a man's neck.

Mark looked around the gym. It was two stories high and about thirty feet square. There were no spectators. The attendants who brought the equipment had vanished through another door. Only the two shotgun guards, one on each door, remained. The Preacher took off his bulky shirt and pants, then laced on a pair of high-top, well-worn basketball shoes. A pair of gym shorts completed his fighting costume.

The two men with the pump shotguns grinned at the preparations, sure of the outcome. Mark swung the stick a little, trying to warm up. He hadn't touched a quarter staff for years.

"Are you ready, my small optimistic opponent? I will endeavor not to injure you beyond repair. I'd say one broken arm or leg should suffice to win the wager."

"Agreed," Mark said. His only problem was that now he had three targets, three opponents. Somehow he had to take out at least one of the shotgun guards in the heat of battle before he put the big man down. And he must be able to position himself near the second shotgun man so he could deal with him quickly.

Preacher jumped into the center of the cleared area and roared like a bull moose and Mark laughed.

"Ready?"

"Ready."

Preacher charged. Mark moved backward, circled to the left, working the quarter staff with both hands on it two feet apart, flicking the ends at the big man, blocking his own shots, working closer and closer to the wall where one of the guards stood. The Preacher was good with the stick, and Mark could probably still take him out without using kendo. But kendo would be faster. Mark saw the shotgun guard start to move out of the path of the fight and Mark knew he had to make a try at him now. He slid his hands to the end of the staff and swung it like a baseball bat at the giant in front of him. But the swing still came in such a way there could be no true counter attack and no blocking. Retreat was the only book answer, and Preacher wisely jumped back easily out of the stick's path. Mark continued his swing, wrapping his hands over his head. He jumped backward at the same time the staff slammed into the shotgun guard. The heavy side of the stick caught the guard in the chest, caving in a rib, knocking him down and putting him out of action. He passed out from the broken rib which punctured his lung.

Mark advanced now with a bayonet charge scream that amused the big man, who quickly blocked Mark's advance.

Just as suddenly Mark changed his tactics. He took the staff like a samurai sword. Now the attack was with a series of thrusts, stabs, quick and sure, that could not all be countered with the lumbering double-handed staff. Mark thudded the tip of the blunt pole against Preacher's ribs and heard him grunt. The next thrust grazed the big man's jaw but did little damage.

Preacher's confident smile faded. His bald head began to bead with sweat. He was confused, not ready for such unorthodox movements, and it threw off his timing. Mark took a stinging blow on the thigh but the power had been dissipated when the staff was half parried with the double-handed samurai movement.

Mark moved around the Preacher's staff, slammed his own weapon into the Preacher's neck, withdrew and stabbed his stomach. The blow was solid and hurt the big man. Preacher jumped back, his eyes alert now, wary, angry. He drove in quickly, determined to take one blow but to get close enough to give a better one in return, a counterpunch that he counted on to end the contest. But Mark would not be drawn into that kind of tradeoff. He kept clipping Preacher in damaging thrusts, but did not blast through the partial defense with his own disabling blow. He wasn't ready yet.

The contest waged on. Mark could sense the big man tiring. It had been five minutes, and Mark figured Preacher liked short, quick battles. Mark needed to work him closer to the other shotgun guard, who had not come to his partner's aid, but let him lie sprawled on the floor.

Mark turned and purposefully stumbled but made a show of it, doing a roll on his shoulder and coming up within ten feet of the second guard. Preacher Mann was on him in a rush, caution gone now, driving in for the broken arm, or head. He fought with a sudden zeal, concentrating on finishing the battle and being the victor just as quickly as he could.

Mark's jab with the staff brought blood to Preacher's nose, then a slash just missed and Preacher countered with the swung tip of his own staff which grazed Mark's head. The stinging blow was not damaging and Mark saw his opening. He thrust, then brought the staff down hard on the side of the big man's neck. A smaller, weaker person would have suffered a broken neck, but it would at least put the Preacher down and out. Mark saw the man's eyes glazing and knew he was half unconscious already. Mark turned and, in one quick motion, threw his staff like a javelin, straight at the surprised shotgun guard ten feet away who had his weapon at port arms. He'd never needed it in here before.

The long staff flew straight and true. The blunt tip hit the right side of the guard's chest, tore through shirt and flesh, caved in two ribs, and penetrated the red pulp of his lung before it crashed through two more ribs in back and exited through the guards shirt.

Mark rushed to the fallen man, stripped the shotgun from his hands and checked the rounds. One was chambered and the safety was off. He charged for the gym door. Almost no one was in the corridors. Quickly Mark retraced his path to Joanna's room, where the door was locked. Three hard kick from Mark's heavy boot splintered the lock and rammed open the door.

"Come on, we've got to get out of this place." They turned toward the door. Two guards ran up. Mark's first round from the shotgun blew them both backward across the corridor before they could reach for their guns. Mark and Joanna ran past them. The sound of the shotgun brought other guards, but none of these had guns, only short electrified night sticks.

Mark ran past the guards, holding Joanna's hand, waving the shotgun at anyone who even looked at them. They came to the cryogenic cells, and even fewer people. They kept running and here and there they saw a human frozen form in the cells. At the far end of this corridor they discovered no one else was around them.

Now and then they heard voices over the loudspeakers recessed in the corridors every twenty feet. Mark checked the area, and saw he had not been here before. The place was marked Level B, Aisle 3. The loudspeaker came on over their heads.

"Congratulations, Mr. Penetrator. You are good. You surprised me and functioned with the staff in a highly unconventional and potent manner I did not expect. But now the game is over. Either you report in that you have decided to join me, or the beautiful Joanna Tabler and yourself have only a very few minutes to live. Unfortunately we have no automatic weapons covering that area, since no weapons are permitted in the delicate cryogenic zones, or in Aisle 3, Level B where you now are. But we have other means of dealing with you. It is now exactly 3:58 A.M. In two minutes all of the oxygen will be shut off to your area and the remaining air in that sector will be pumped out. All of our own personnel have been evacuated to safe zones. The sector will clear in six minutes and after that you have perhaps another two to live.

"Phone from the small communicator directly across from any speaker, and your life will be spared. Remember, Penetrator, if you don't phone, now, you have only seven minutes to live."

## Chapter 16

# BIG CRYOGENIC SMASHUP

Mark grabbed Joanna's hand and pulled her with him. as he stormed the last fifty feet to the end of the corridor. There had to be some of the escape hatches he'd seen from the outside. Where were they? How did they appear? The end of the tunnel was blank, no door, no hatch, nothing but a rock wall. Mark moved back along the corridor testing the walls, checking them, watching for tubes, wires.

He found a suspicious place just past the second loudspeaker. Mark checked his watch and saw that it was precisely 4:00 A.M. The speaker hummed into operation.

"It is now 4:00 A.M., Mr. Penetrator and Miss Tabler. I'm truly sorry that you have not seen your way clear to join us in our operation here in Florida. So, good-bye. The pumps will start in fifteen seconds."

There was a pause, then a new voice came over the speaker system.

"Attention. Attention! We have a first-class red alert

159

in the cryogenics section. Will all qualified refrigeration technicians report at once to the refrigerant section on each floor. Our digital readouts show a massive breakdown in the deuterium circulation systems. Please report at once."

Mark grinned. "That's my new friend at work downstairs, which might be enough to mess up their time table on clobbering us. Hey, are you cold?"

Joanna laughed and nodded. "You finally noticed. But I'm glad to be out of that room, and I've never been so glad to see anyone in my life. How did you find me? Where did you come from? Was this your mission all along? You know they were going to freeze me, make me into an icicle."

"That's one icicle I wouldn't mind chewing on. Now, enough of this. Where is that damn vent? Mark tapped the butt of the shotgun against the wall where he saw the wire vanish, but it was solid rock.

Where would the vents, the hatches, be? He and Joanna raced away from the end of the tunnel, all the time Mark expecting some sliding partition to come hurtling across the corridor, cutting off their retreat, setting up the section to be exhausted of air. It didn't happen. They came to a short cross corridor and ran to the end of it. This time Mark found one of the things he was looking for: a stairwell leading downward.

"Come on, he'll look for us going up. We go down and find the guts of this place, the hard iron, the machinery, the power-house if we can. He's got to have some generators and pumps and probably diesel or turbine engines down here somewhere."

The steel steps led downward a story and a half, then Mark saw a second jungle of pipes, big engines, turbines, shafts and electrical leads, enough to run a city. He recognized some of it: three huge gas turbine engines whining away at peak load and speed driving in-place generators.

A man came around the corner of the masses of tubing and pipes, a heavy wrench held in his hand.

"Thought I heard something. Who the hell are you two?" His eyes bulged as he stared at Joanna's nakedness. She moved behind Mark.

Mark brought up the shotgun to cover the man who stood twenty feet away.

"Who are we? I'm the guy who's about to blow your head off if you don't drop the weapon."

The man tossed the wrench to the floor.

"Now, who are you? You work here?"

"Yes, right. I'm a half-assed guard and technician. I watch the dials and gauges and make sure everything works right."

"You know what's happening upstairs?"

"Sure, they're trying to freeze dogs and cats and bring them back to life. Everyone knows that."

"And they're now freezing people. Did you know that?"

"My God! Is that true?"

"Yes." Mark was looking at the turbines and their matched generator sets. They all fed through one group of cables into a bank of transformers.

"Ever tried to get off this rock?"

"No, they pay me well."

"But are you one of the hard-core types? Do you have a criminal record?"

"Of course not, I'm a technician."

Mark heard him and stared at the electrical output again, then at another whole row of pumps. They needed the pumps to drain out the sea water seepage. Nearly half the complex must be under sea level, so the pumps were vital. Which gave him something of a problem. The generators were a primary target, but so were the pumps. And he couldn't blow them both with the one charge detonator he had left. He looked at the young man across the aisle.

"How do those pumps operate? Do they have an independent power source?"

"Those? Hell, no. Work from the main power supply like everything else."

That solved Mark's problem. He pulled up the sleeve on his right arm and stripped off the C-5 sheet plastique with its protective wrapper and its detonator/timer. He went to the point where the power from all three generators fed into a huge transformer and looked at the insulated leads. All the Power from the three generators passed through this one small point! He wrapped the C-5 around the big cable and inserted the timer/detonator, set it for thirty seconds and activated it.

The three of them ran for the far corner of the big room behind some sturdy pumps and a short wall. Shortly after they got there the C-5 detonated, shattering the silence with a snapping roar that rattled around the big room, making it seem like they were sitting inside a giant bass drum during a parade.

Mark jumped to his feet first, ordered the guard to take off his shirt. He did so. "Now the pants, off with them. Come on, we don't have all day!" He gave the shirt to Joanna who put it on with a smile. The pants were too big for her, but at least she was covered and much warmer.

"Now, you had better get top side," Mark told the

guard. "This whole place is about ready to go stale and blow right out of the Atlantic. You know the quickest way out of here?"

"Yeah, this way. It goes out the back."

The Penetrator studied the man for just a moment, decided he was too frightened to lie and followed him in his undershirt and shorts up the steel ladder and back to the level they just left. The guard ran to a speaker on the wall, moved it aside and pulled a concealed handle. One four-foot section of the corridor wall began to swing inward. It got halfway to the floor and the electrical motor which moved it ground to a halt.

"Batteries are surging," the technician said. They looked past the wall section and saw that it opened directly outside. Mark stepped out. It was the lower side of the island, about thirty meters from the water. He caught Joanna's hand and helped her out. Then he jumped back inside.

"Joanna, you stay right out there until I come and get you. I've got to take care of the Preacher."

Mark grabbed the guard. "How well do you know this place?"

"I helped build it. I've been here two years."

"Good. Now show me where Preacher would retreat if something started going wrong. Is there a secret escape tunnel or a private bastion he has somewhere?"

"I don't think so. I never saw it. Just that big office."

"Take me there."

Mark checked and saw he had four more shots in the scatter gun. He and the guard ran along the corridor, changed directions. There were few people.

They met two guards with shock sticks, but they cowed back from Mark's shotgun. The cryogenic cells looked dim and somehow limp, as if the refrigerant indeed had been cut off. But if left closed they would maintain their low temperature for hours.

Mark saw a white-coated doctor, who screamed at him and ran the other way. They went up one flight of steps and Mark saw that many of the lights in the corridor had blinked out. Only half were now working.

"The whole electrical system is dual, on two sets of batteries," the guard said. "If one set of batteries goes out, the others come on so we have half-light at any time. But they'll all run down in twenty minutes without the input of those turbine generators."

Ahead, someone fired a shot. A bullet whistled past Mark. He jumped behind an open office doorway and pulled the guard down with him. There were cryogenic cells all around them, and Mark wondered who had broken the rule and fired. He peered around the metal door but saw the corridor was clear ahead.

Mark touched the guard's shoulder. "Look, you said you're not one of the hard core idiots here."

"Hell no. I work for the pay. I don't know what goes on in these medical floors. I don't want to know."

"You can help me, then, and help yourself. You know where those ten girls are locked up, the pretty prostitutes?" The kid nodded. "Go and break down the door and let them out. Tell them to get to the surface out one of the escape hatches. Lead them out."

"Yeah, that I can do."

"But first, is there some kind of emergency system, used for danger, for explosions, for refrigerant leaks, anything like that?"

"Yeah. They call them the panic buttons. Should be one on each floor. Get fired if you push it and nothing is wrong. Lost my best buddy that way. He was plastered and he. . . ."

Mark put his hand over the kid's mouth. "You know where one is, and can you push it and stay alive?"

"Sure, no sweat."

"Okay, then you do it, and get the girls out, but first tell me how I get to the big man's office."

"Right down to the end of the corridor, and turn right. Then it's straight ahead. There's a reception desk out front. The guy there has some nasty tools. Be careful of him and don't get too close."

"Right. Now hit the alarm and then get the girls out of here."

The loudspeaker system came on in what sounded like a prerecorded message.

"Warning, warning. The electrical system is on standby. We have a total of ten minutes of power left in the wet-cell battery banks."

The speaker snapped off.

Before Mark could move, another voice came over the sound system.

"For God's sakes, somebody get down to refrigeration on Sub-Level C. This place looks like it's been wrecked by a maniac. Half of it is smashed up. Valves are opened, lines broken. It's going to take six months to get this place functioning again. Somebody come down here and help me!"

Mark ran down the vacant corridor. He saw the softer lights, turned the corner and far ahead he saw the reception desk in the middle of the aisle. He moved toward it slowly, trying not to be seen, moving from office to office. No one seemed to be around anymore. There must be some built-in automatic protection ahead. He looked at the entrance from fifty feet away and saw a clue. Concealed guns of some kind on each side of the desk seemed like a possiblity. They would be about ten feet in front and aimed to crossfire at an angle outward. If they missed the victim, they went into carefully arranged shot absorbing walls. A targetlike small rug had been placed six feet in front of the desk, acting as a psychological landing spot for anyone coming to talk. Perfectly oriented for quick removal.

The speakers came alive again.

"The pumps can no longer keep out the salt water in Level C. We're in danger of losing the whole Level C cryogenic holding cells. Extreme danger. Suggest we shunt all available power to Level C for pumping action. If the sea water hits those absolute zero frozen cells down here, each one is going to blow up like a box of nitrogclycerin! Get us some power down here, damnit!"

Just as he finished speaking a wailing siren sound filled the corridor. Mark saw heads pop out of offices near the receptionist. The man at the desk stood, wonder on his face.

One person hurried past Mark heading for a cross corridor. He carried a small briefcase and a worried expression. Three more men came from offices and went past the receptionist and through back doors, evidently heading out.

The siren kept surging up and down. A dozen more people rushed past Mark now, some white-coated medics included. All were men. The only women Mark had seen on the island were the victims— hookers and Joanna.

More workers came past. No one paid any attention to Mark now. Suddenly the siren cut off. The voice that followed it was stern, commanding. It was Preacher Mann.

"No one will leave his post. The siren was not authorized. There is an emergency, but not a disaster. Everyone must hold his post, do his job, and we will make repairs just as quickly as we can. We have doubled our battery supply and power will hold now for another thirty minutes. All functions are in order except the cryogenics. All life support is solid and sure. There is no danger to any personnel. Remain at your posts!"

The loudspeaker shut off and Mark knew there would be no more panic use of it by underlings. He walked toward the receptionist. When he was just inside the carpeted area he knew the man had seen him. Mark lifted the shotgun from beside his leg and felt a bullet puncture the air beside him. The guy was firing through the desk! Mark blasted a shot at the man then dove toward the wall, rolled and came up with a new shell chambered and ready to fire. A few of the tiny pellets from the scattergun had stained the man's forehead. One penetrated his left eyeball. The receptionist stood waving an Uzi machine gun, trying to find a target.

Mark shot again, the buckshot splattering the man's chest, slapping him backward six feet, tearing the life from his body in one massive blood wave.

The Penetrator was on his feet, running. He scooped up the Uzi, checked the magazine, then went into the same door where he had been taken earlier, but found it empty. Which door next? He remembered and stood to one side of the door and turned the knob. As the handle moved, a dozen slugs roared and splintered through the door, chest high. The door swung open.

"So it's down to this, is it, Mr. Penetrator," Preacher Mann said. "I saw you take out George on my TV monitor. Ingenious, and some good shooting. But the Uzi won't help you now." The lights dimmed, went out, came back on.

"Only a shift over to the backup batteries, my small friend. Your old ally, darkness, will not aid you this time."

Then the lights went out and the inside of the island was as black as anything Mark had ever experienced. There was absolutely *no* outside illumination, and no artificial light of any kind. Mark's *Sho-tu-ça* had remained on full force through the attack, and now he utilized his heightened hearing to Pinpoint the movements of the big man in the next room. At first he heard nothing. His night vision did not help him since there was no light at all which he could magnify.

Mark waited, and at last heard deep breathing, then the squeak of a chair. The big man was moving. Mark remembered the layout of the large office. The two doors on the far side. He pointed the Uzi around the doorway and sprayed six rounds into the room. At once he heard a screech of pain, then a long sigh. Was it over? Had that been the death scream of Preacher.Mann and the end of all his demonic plans?

## Chapter 17

# FLOAT ONE, BLAST TWO

The Penetrator did not move. He held his breath, ears straining to pick up the slightest sound from the next room. After almost a minute he heard an exhaled breath, a knee crack, then running steps, a crash of furniture. Mark moved into the room after him. A door slammed. Mark stumbled into a chair, then found the door. Was it the right one?

He dove through it into blackness. Not a flicker of light. Sounds all around him, people, people shuffling, whispering. A match flared and he saw it fifty feet down the corridor. One match led to others, then cigarette lighters. Forms walked slowly toward expected exits.

Suddenly the lights came back on. A dozen persons in the corridor put hands over their eyes. It was painful. No one could see anything for sixty to ninety seconds, then gradually vision returned.

Mark waved the machine gun under the nearest person's face.

"Which way did Preacher Mann go? He just came through here. Which way was he headed?"

The man pointed down the long hallway. Mark checked three more people, all who directed him the same way. He got to the stairs and someone said the Preacher had gone running down that way moments before.

Where was he going?

Mark ran down the steps cautiously, opened the door and stared down the corridor. It was Level C. Water seeped into the floor, an inch, two inches deep. It hadn't reached the cryogenic cells yet where they were built up a foot off the floor. Mark saw the big black man at the far end of the corridor. The Penetrator snapped off a four-round burst, but even as he lifted the weapon, Preached Mann ducked into a doorway. The spray of hot lead missed him.

"You'll never get me now, Mr. Penetrator!" Preacher shouted. "See who I've got with me?"

As Mark looked the fifty feet down the aisle, the big man pulled Joanna from a room.

"Now isn't this cozy?" Preacher said. "I got your lady love, and when this sea water gets another foot higher, this place will blow up like a fourth of July firewords wagon. My experts tell me the salt water will explode when it hits the super chill of the absolute zero cells. The cells will then form a chain reaction, exploding one after the next until this little island will look like Jackass Flats on nuke day. The water's coming in slow now, Penetrator, but all I have to do is hit this one valve and salt water will storm in here like a geyser. We're twenty feet below sea level."

Mark zeroed in on the Preacher but, before he

could squeeze the trigger on single shot, the big man pulled Joanna in front of him.

"My small opponent, you must wonder how I got Joanna so quickly. My topside guards saw you come out, but by the time they got there you re-entered the complex, so they brought Joanna directly to me through the main entrance. Much quicker than the route you used."

"Preacher, let go of her or I'll shoot up the cryogenic cell beside you. The gases will escape and Joanna will be able to run up here."

"Mr. Penetrator, you're forgetting your Logic 101 class. Shame. I may take away your degree. You must know by now that you simply can't have it both ways. You want to see this young lady alive, you must come and get her and then try for the surface before the cryogenic nightmare down here begins. If you don't make it you're both dead, dead, dead. But it's up to you. If you want me dead that intensely, just start blasting away, you'll get me, but Joanna will suffer an untimely death as well with a knife in her heart. I used to be quite good with a blade, and they say you never lose the touch."

Mark hesitated. He did want them both—Preacher dead and Joanna alive. The big black man used the doorway's protection as he pulled on a scuba tank and adjusted the straps, examined the valves and face plate. He tied Joanna to the door handle.

"You might have time to get her and make it back out the way we came down, but I doubt it." The Preacher laughed. "I do know that you're going to try, otherwise we both would have been dead by now. Don't worry about me. I'll be out and gone before you can get here. There's a floodable room in here but it works only once, so don't try to follow me. I'll have a long enjoyable swim this morning. Oh, I'm used to it. We'll probably meet again, Penetrator, and next time it will be my turn to be the winner."

He was gone. Mark ran down the slippery corridor. The water was now less than three inches from the cryogenic cell floors. There had to be time!

The water was eight or nine inches deep as he slipped and skidded to Joanna. He tore at the bindings, wishing he had a knife. At last the tie came free and both began the long trip back down the corridor. They tried to run, but that sloshed water against the Plexiglas walls of the cryogenic cells. One began to steam, another sputtered as if it were a hot stove hit with water drops. They slowed.

"Easy now, we're not sure if the cells will explode or not when the water hits them. Nobody has ever tried it. It might get a foot deep on the outside wall before enough seeps through to do any damage. We don't even know if these cells are the ones at absolute zero degrees."

Joanna slowed, then overcompensated and slipped and splashed into the water. Her arms flailed the air and Mark couldn't catch her. A wave of water a foot high sloshed against one of the cryogenic cells. The clear water wall splintered, cracked and sucked inward, shattering in an implosion that made almost no noise but was followed at once by an explosion as the salt water hit the cryonic cold floor of the cell.

It was like one stick of dynamite going off in a cave, Mark thought as he got to his feet from the water where the blast had knocked him down. He couldn't hear a thing. His head rang and spun and he grabbed Joanna and ran. They let the water splash on the walls, ran with more luck than skill as they slashed through the foot of water.

"Come on, just another fifteen yards!" Mark shouted.

Behind them something exploded. The lights flickered. The tubelike gun barrel corridor funneled the shock wave directly at Mark and Joanna, slamming them forward, knocking them down, skidding them along the floor to the stairwell door. They scrambled to their feet, pulled open the heavy metal door and splashed through to the stairway. Behind them another thundering explosion hit and rattled the door.

"Upstairs, quickly!" Mark yelled, realizing neither of them could hear the words. They ran up the steps, Joanna held back by the wet, baggy, too-big pants. Mark grabbed her hand, pulling her with him.

The lights flickered again. They came out on Level B and Mark looked for an open hatchway. He was sure many of the workers must have used them. None were open. Furiously he pushed aside a speaker. There was no handle behind it. He ran to four of the speakers before he found one with an exit handle. Mark pulled it and slowly a four-foot escape hatch ground back from the wall. Mark and Joanna jumped through it before it was fully opened. Just then the whole island shook with a dozen thunderous explosions. Geysers of water jetted into the sky for fifty feet. The water boiled and hissed and when it quieted, bits and pieces of ceiling tile and furniture showed in the rolling sea water. That was the end of Level C.

Mark and Joanna looked toward the top of the small island. More than a hundred people crowded on the hill, staying as far away from the underwater sections as possible.

It took Mark a moment to realize that it was dawn. The sun was almost up, the sky a muddy gray with wisps of fog and a few clouds. Daylight was coming quickly.

Mark caught Joanna's hand, then picked her up when he remembered she had no shoes to protect her feet from the sharp rocks. He carried her toward the small cove where Mark hoped the motorboat lay hidden. Their hearing had returned as the shock wore off.

Joanna put her arms around Mark's neck and kissed his cheek.

"How does a girl say thank you for saving her life?"

Mark grinned, running easily for the cove. "She can forget about desserts so she doesn't gain another five pounds," he said. She kissed his cheek again.

The boat was still there, intact, undiscovered. Mark pushed it out and turned it carefully so the others on the hill wouldn't hear them. Then he started the engine, let it warm up for ten seconds before spurting over the top of a submerged rock and shot through the opening in the reef and into the green Atlantic.

It took Mark and Joanna half an hour to cross to the mainland, and then they worked down the coast to West Palm Beach. They slid the boat in at the same marina where Mark had "borrowed" it, and walked away without attracting attention. The guard at the gate barely looked up as they left. It wasn't his job to question those who came out of the marina, only those who tried to get in.

On the street Mark chuckled. He had his car keys, over four thousand dollars in his money belt, but not a thin dime for a phone call. Mark found the Mustang parked where he had left it, and then went to three stores before he talked someone into making change for his hundred dollar bill.

Mark called the coast guard and made his report using a fictitious name. He said he had seen explosions and fire out of a little island just off the coast, and that there were dozens of persons in distress there. He suggested that a cutter or a plane take a look there immediately. Mark hung up before they could ask for any details.

Mark sagged. He felt like he was a thousand years old and hadn't slept for half that long. He struggled back to the car, knowing he needed to recuperate.

# EPILOGUE

Joanna lay in the sun near their rented beach cottage, applying sun-screen lotion to her lovely body. Mark slept in the shade nearby, his body winning its fight to recoup its massive energy drain of the past forty-eight hours.

They both knew that first morning that it would be far too dangerous to go back to Joanna's hotel for her suitcases, so they turned and drove up the coast until they found an inconspicuous and out of the way beach cottage for rent and took it for two weeks, cash in advance. Joanna went to a small shopping center and came back with "emergency" materials such as makeup and a few simple sun clothes and a sack of food. The next day she bought more necessities and some sports clothes, then she settled down to watch and help Mark recuperate. She knew about how long it would take for his body to regenerate after the tremendous physical drain brought on by a mission like this.

Mark determined that his arm had not been broken after all by the smash of the quarter staff. His ribs were cracked and would take time to heal. The bruise there was deep and sore where the bullet had been turned away by the Resistweve cloth. The other bullet bruise on his shoulder wasn't as bad, but he would remember it every time he moved for at least two weeks.

The ribs hurt more this time than when he had broken them before, he was sure. Or was it that he knew what to expect this time? He could take some pain pills, but he shied away from them. He would gut it out. Mark was sold on the use of Resistweve cloth, and hoped that every cop and detective in the country soon had shirt and pants made of it. He was going to set up some sort of a promotional fund for the inventor of the cloth as soon as he got back to the Stronghold.

Joanna had watched the TV news reports that first evening. There was complete coverage including pictures of some still-frozen animals. There were no pictures of frozen humans, and the reporters only hinted that such work had been done experimentally there. Camera crews went into the A and B levels but the C level was totally destroyed and submerged. There were no reports about finding the man behind it all, now plainly declared to be Preacher Mann, the mastermind of the whole program.

One of the workers at the island, a refrigeration technician, told about the one-man army who had talked with him, and how he had devastated the whole complex. The reporters quickly tied it in with the Penetrator and his attack on the rooftop the night before.

Mark called the professor from a pay phone the same day they rented the cottage, gave a quick report and said not even to think about contacting him for a month, then he changed that to two weeks.

Joanna phoned Dan Griggs, who was out. She left a message with his secretary reporting that Preacher Mann's power base was totally destroyed and that he was out of business. She said that Mann had escaped but didn't spell it out.

Mark rolled over, groaned when his ribs stabbed him and sat up.

"Hey, Joanna, just how did it feel sitting there naked in that chair and knowing that within forty-eight hours you might make history by being the first defrosted cryonic woman?"

She threw a book at him and they both laughed. Then they settled down to getting reacquainted. They had a lot to catch up on, including their delayed plans for a vacation together in Maui in Hawaii. Joanna went for a swim in the surf and Mark watched her.

As he saw her playing in the breakers, he thought about a problem that had been bothering him for some time now—the increased possibility of biological warfare. There was the old story of how the army had experimented with "nondangerous" but "slightly toxic" materials and cultures on civilians in years past. Then the Legionaire's disease had left the population gasping in surprise and shock for six months before an actual cause was pinned down.

Lately Mark and the professor had been discovering more and more reports of unusual diseases striking in the most unlikely spots. In seemed to be much more than coincidence, and in each case there had been no determination whatsoever of how the cultures of diseases had suddenly cropped up in these sections of the United States. Was some foreign power using the nation as a test tube for biological and germ warfare experiments?

Mark started to roll over, but his sore ribs stopped him. In two weeks the ribs would be healed enough to forget, but right now they pained with his every movement.

So for now he would think ribs, not germ warfare or chemical depopulation. Right now he wanted to ease off and relax, to enjoy for a short time the life of a normal man, with nobody sighting a weapon at him and trying to kill him. Yes, glorious peace—for a few short days and nights.

# THE PENETRATOR

### by Lionel Derrick

Mark Hardin. Discharged from the army, after service in Vietnam. His military career was over. But *his* war was just beginning. His reason for living and reason for dying became the same—to stamp out crime and corruption wherever he finds it. He is deadly; he is unpredictable; and he is dedicated. He is The Penetrator!

Read all of him in:

| Order | | Title | Book No. | Price |
|---|---|---|---|---|
| _____ | # 1 | THE TARGET IS H | P236 | $ .95 |
| _____ | # 2 | BLOOD ON THE STRIP | P237 | $ .95 |
| _____ | # 3 | CAPITOL HELL | P318 | $ .95 |
| _____ | # 4 | HIJACKING MANHATTAN | P338 | $ .95 |
| _____ | # 5 | MARDI GRAS MASSACRE | P378 | $ .95 |
| _____ | # 6 | TOKYO PURPLE | P434 | $1.25 |
| _____ | # 7 | BAJA BANDIDOS | P502 | $1.25 |
| _____ | # 8 | THE NORTHWEST CONTRACT | P540 | $1.25 |
| _____ | # 9 | DODGE CITY BOMBERS | P627 | $1.25 |
| _____ | #10 | THE HELLBOMB FLIGHT | P690 | $1.25 |

**TO ORDER**

Please check the space next to the book/s you want, send this order form together with your check or money order, include the price of the book/s and 25¢ for handling and mailing, to:

PINNACLE BOOKS, INC. / P.O. Box 4347
Grand Central Station / New York, N. Y. 10017

☐ Check here if you want a free catalog.

I have enclosed $_____ check_____ or money order_____ as payment in full. No C.O.D.'s.

Name_____

Address_____

City_____ State_____ Zip_____
(Please allow time for delivery)

# THE INCREDIBLE ACTION PACKED SERIES

# DEATH MERCHANT

## by Joseph Rosenberger

His name is Richard Camellion, he's a master of disguise, deception and destruction. He does what the CIA and FBI cannot do.

| Order | | Title | Book # | Price |
|---|---|---|---|---|
| ___ | #1 | THE DEATH MERCHANT | P211 | $ .95 |
| ___ | #2 | OPERATION OVERKILL | P245 | $ .95 |
| ___ | #3 | THE PSYCHOTRON PLOT | P117 | $ .95 |
| ___ | #4 | CHINESE CONSPIRACY | P168 | $ .95 |
| ___ | #5 | SATAN STRIKE | P182 | $ .95 |
| ___ | #6 | ALBANIAN CONNECTION | P670 | $1.25 |
| ___ | #7 | CASTRO FILE | P264 | $ .95 |
| ___ | #8 | BILLIONAIRE MISSION | P339 | $ .95 |
| ___ | #9 | THE LASER WAR | P399 | $ .95 |
| ___ | #10 | THE MAINLINE PLOT | P473 | $1.25 |
| ___ | #11 | MANHATTAN WIPEOUT | P561 | $1.25 |
| ___ | #12 | THE KGB FRAME | P642 | $1.25 |
| ___ | #13 | THE MATO GROSSO HORROR | P705 | $1.25 |
| ___ | #14 | VENGEANCE OF THE GOLDEN HAWK | P796 | $1.25 |
| ___ | #15 | THE IRON SWASTIKA PLOT | P823 | $1.25 |
| ___ | #16 | INVASION OF THE CLONES | P857 | $1.25 |
| ___ | #17 | THE ZEMLYA EXPEDITION | P880 | $1.25 |